I0771021

A SLIGHTLY STRANGER POINT OF VIEW © 2025 Hannah Birss

Published by Graveside Press
graveside-press.com

Editing: Kelley York
Cover illustration: BC Maxwell at Illumax
Interior Formatting: Sleepy Fox Studio

Digital 978-1-967547-23-4
Paperback (KDP) 978-1-967547-20-3
Paperback (Trade) 978-1-967547-21-0
Hardcover 978-1-967547-22-7

A SLIGHTLY STRANGER POINT OF VIEW

HANNAH BIRSS

CONTENT NOTES

Please note: because this is a horror anthology, it should be assumed that the basic horror tropes will apply.
These include death, gore, and violence.

For a list of potentially triggering subjects, please refer to page 196.

THE PIPER

From the Desk of "Father" Jester, Concerning the Events that Occurred in The Town of Hamelin, Lower Saxony, On the 26th of June in the Year of Our Lord 1284

WE SHOULD HAVE paid attention when the rats began to disappear.

I could be forgiven for my ignorance at the beginning. At the time, I lived alone in a small, forgotten shack on the very outskirts of the town. My home was close to the Weser River, and I did my best to limit my exposure to the townsfolk of Hamelin and the casual cruelty they aimed at me.

They called me Jester—not because they thought I was possessed of a sense of humor or particular wit, but because I was hideous to look at and this amused the townsfolk. My appearance was not the result of a terrible accident, unless you count the accident of birth. I assume I came forth from my mother's womb with this affliction, as I was placed on the doorstep of the church as a newborn, my face sagging, my left side weak and barely able to move. Half of my face hangs numbly, without a semblance of strength or movement. My eye droops, and while I eventually managed to learn how to walk, it was with one foot dragging slightly behind me and my back

hunched. I had focused on building up the muscle in my arm, and so have full use of it, though it sits at an awkward angle to my body.

I grew up as a foundling raised by the church in the attached monastery. There, I learned my letters through careful observation, and quickly became able to read and write. Though many of the monks looked upon me with disdain, the abbot took me under his wing and nurtured my love for God as well as for the written word. After he died, several unfortunate circumstances occurred in tandem around the monastery, and I made an appropriate scapegoat. The new head of the monastery tossed me out onto the streets at the tender age of twelve. There, I fashioned myself clothes from the cast-offs of the village, a pied outfit roughly sewn and cobbled together that only cemented the nickname I had carried with me since birth. Now, I cannot remember the name the abbot had originally given me. I'm sure that it was something appropriately pious. All that is left to me is Jester, and so Jester I am.

The disappearance and departure of the rats did not happen all at once. A few households remarked within my earshot on how the plague of rodents in their households had seemed reduced, as if the tide was finally beginning to turn in the constant war against the vermin. There were no bodies, no ominous signs, nothing to arouse suspicion. There were simply fewer of them.

I saw a strange exodus of them once. I had gone to the river to fill my old waterskin, and there stood a group of people at the muddy edge, broken apart into two sides like the Red Sea. Between them poured a horde of rats, running and writhing and falling all over each other in their rush to escape the town. They went into the water as they fled to the opposite bank of the Weser, swimming with their small arms flailing and their long bald tails swishing behind them like rudders. The noise—the panicked squeaks, the sounds of their claws scrabbling at the rocky ground—was overwhelming to my ears. I lingered further downstream, only creeping closer when I saw that the people were adequately distracted by the tide of vermin.

The townsfolk talked amongst themselves as they watched—the same things said over and over, a call and response that didn't contribute anything to the conversation. I tuned them out, observing the rats with a growing sense of dread. I could not put my finger on what made me so uneasy; it was different, and different was usually a sign of something bad, something to be aware of, a concept that had been ingrained into me long ago. The monks and townsfolk had seen to that.

To prove the point, a nearby villager elbowed his companion in the ribs, pointing in my direction. They turned toward me, sneers on their faces.

"Why don't you run into the river with them, Jester?" one of them mocked. "Do us all a favor?" His friend leaned down, snatching a dirty rock and whipping it at me.

I made a hasty retreat, slinking away as they continued to hurl their taunts and rocks, which stung against my hunched back. Their words themselves did not bother me; I had long ago developed both a literally and figuratively thick skin. To them, I was a hideous creature and therefore could not possibly be a man of reason or worthy of basic respect. However, injury was a very real worry of mine. With my own ailments and physical disabilities, combined with the solitary nature of my existence, any true injury or resulting infection could have disastrous, life-ending consequences.

I still should have told someone about that first odd night. I was wandering—searching for food or bits of clothing left abandoned in the streets or refuse piles, walking along the river's edge and down dim alleys. I preferred not to be visible during the day for obvious reasons, and the blanket of darkness afforded me comfort and safe passage. I was moving slowly, my eyes scanning back and forth, when I realized that I was not alone.

Another figure—tall, long and lean, a shadow lingering at the edges of human habitation— moved slowly through the streets, peering behind old clutter and moving aside piles of rubbish, frustration evident in every jagged, angry movement. In hindsight, I believe he was looking for the rats.

He moved to a window and made as if to open it. I called out sternly then, hoping to interrupt whatever nefarious plan he had in mind. It was then that he turned to me. No, not he—*it*, for it was not a man, not truly.

It was tall, much taller than I. Its limbs were disproportionate to its body, and its long white fingers reminded me of spider legs wrapping around a windowsill. It was ghostly pale, mouth large, reminding me of a carp—a wide, grim slash in the middle of its face. Its eyes caught my own, and they burned with a strange yellow fire.

The blood in my veins turned to ice. It must have been a *nachzehrer*, a revenant. Later, I would learn many other names that the creature went by—*strigoi, nosferatu, shtriga, vampire.*

I began to back away slowly. In a methodical manner, it stalked toward me. Its eyes bored into mine. From its lips spilled a simple tune: three long notes hummed over and over again. I could make myself move no further. Within my head I heard a song, a complicated rising and falling, a melody that merged with the humming, overlapping one another until I found myself with no control over my body. I was trapped within the music, so wrapped up in its song that I couldn't even think to pray.

He took a few final steps, and a cold hand lifted to cradle my face. Its burning eyes roamed over my twisted features, and it cocked its head. It moved me this way and that, the infernal song holding me tight in its grasp. In my strangeness, I was like a specimen to it—its clammy fingers fluttered over the numb half of my face. At one point, it stuck a finger in my mouth as if I were a horse, the pad of its finger prodding at my teeth and the inside of my cheeks. I followed its every move, examining it as it examined me. It was fascinating and terrifying to behold.

I did not mean to bite it—the rest of me was still as a statue, but when it poked at a part of my inner cheek it was pure reflex, and my teeth clamped down against its skin, drawing out a thick, viscous fluid that spurted onto my tongue and filled it with the taste of iron and of rot. Its blood was cold. If I could have, I would have spat it out, but I was still an insect caught in the web of a spider and could not move of my own volition. With a hiss, it yanked my long brown hair until my neck was violently exposed. One of its long arms reached around to my lower back, holding me as if I were a lover. I saw a flash of long, sharp teeth before it buried them in my neck. It was excruciatingly painful, yet it was the closest thing to an embrace I had ever known at that point in my life.

When it was finished, it dropped me and turned and strode away. I lay there in the cold mud, blood seeping from the wounds on my neck. I drifted in and out of consciousness, that infernal song vibrating within my skull until the first rays of blessed sun shone their light over the horizon.

At that, the sounds of the music faded away, and I found myself rousing. I dragged myself home, where I fell into a deep sleep that I did not awaken from until the late afternoon.

God forgive me, I did not know what to do at that time. I knew no one would believe me—that no one would believe without evidence that a nachzehrer had taken up residence in the town of Hamelin. In fact, they were far more likely to accuse me of misdeeds or consorting with the devil or some other thin claim and have me burned at the stake. And so, I continued to keep quiet.

Several disappearances were reported in the week that followed— drunken men and women of ill-repute going missing after dark and turning up several days later on the banks of the Weser. The rumor mill was not kind to them; they were all considered the lowest dredges of society, only a step above myself, and so their deaths were met with nothing but a shrug or a mean smirk. Certainly, no one attributed their deaths to a revenant. Only I knew, and years later I can still feel their blood on my hands as my period of inaction lengthened.

Why was I not killed? The question still vexes me. Was I overfull of blood? Was the creature not so hungry as to need to drain me? I slept poorly for those days, always waiting for the nachzehrer to knock on my door and finish its meal, or for the village to come for me as a scapegoat with their pitchforks and torches. Yet neither of them ever did—and as my anxiety grew, I stopped making my journeys into town altogether.

It had been two weeks since my attack, and days since the last drained body washed up. I suppose the nachzehrer grew hungry and impatient. It desired a feast—and so, it made itself one.

One night, as I lay curled in my nest of rags, that same song crept in through the broken window of my squalid home. Unlike last time, I felt no draw to it. It was not meant for me. Gathering my courage, I opened my door a crack to see something approaching from the distance, heading toward the town. As it drew closer, I saw it was a child. Behind it were a few more, all of them occupants of homes in the outlying areas of Hamelin, all of them walking unsteadily on their feet, their eyes glazed and fixed on the horizon. The same three notes, repeated over and over again, echoed through the streets. The song itself came from the bell tower, amplified as the creature sang into the bell.

I slid through the crack in my door and reached out to grasp the shoulder of a young boy as it staggered past me. He shook me off, paid me no heed. I may as well not have been there for all the attention it gave me. The horror of the situation dawned on me. I ran down the road, weaving in and out of the parade of children. As soon as I reached the outskirts of Hamelin, I began to do my best to rouse the townsfolk.

I pounded on doors, not even stopping to see if the people inside had awakened before moving onto the next. People were slow to stir, but I shouted as I went. Parents awoke to find their young children's beds empty. The children marched, deaf to me and their parents, struggling and screaming as people began to pin them down or lift them up. Frantic parents ran through the streets, calling their young ones' names as they roughly turned children around, staring into blank faces.

The song had stopped—the nachzehrer presumably having descended from the bell-tower and moved to the front of the dark procession—but the children continued onwards, in their fugue-like state, listening to music only they and I could hear that led them to the edge of the forest. Someone began to ring the church bells in alarm, adding to the cacophony, as I continued to run through the town, doing my best to wake others. The children stepped purposefully into the dark shadows of the trees, and when their parents tried to follow, the little ones vanished as if ghosts.

After what seemed like hours, but could only have been no more than fifteen minutes, the town had turned from sleep into roaring chaos. The music in my head faded more and more until the children began violently erupting from their hypnotic states. They burst into tears and screamed for their parents, lashing out with their small fists and feet in their confusion.

When dawn broke, the final count was confirmed. Seventy-two children were gone, having followed the revenant into the woods. A great wail went up through the city. The church bells clanged endlessly, and the streets were filled with weeping parents and grieving families. In the town square, hundreds assembled to discuss what had happened and what would be done.

I stood off to the side in an alleyway, silently observing from the shadows so as not to draw attention to myself. After much debate, it was decided the lost children would be considered a sacrifice in the hope that the nachzehrer would be sated and move on.

I couldn't believe what I was hearing, how these parents were so quick to abandon their children. They took God's most precious gift and had decided it was worthy of sacrifice in the vague possibility the nachzehrer would leave them alone. Even the men of the church seemed willing to abandon them, regardless of how the souls of the children were at stake. Instead of rescue, the town began to bustle with spiritual preparations for a potential return, protecting those who were left behind with no thoughts as to the ones that were taken.

I do not wish to speak more on the townsfolk. To this day, I keep a hard place in my heart for them that no amount of prayer or fasting has been able to soften. I had been abandoned as a child. I knew the pain of it, the heartbreak, but I had never been abandoned to a sure death, as these parents had done to their own flesh and blood. I resolved to find them myself and rescue them as I had never been.

It was late morning by the time I returned to my shack. During the previous long nights, I had fashioned myself a series of stakes, whittling endlessly. I collected my makeshift weapons and prayed over them. I went in faith, kissing the weathered cross that hung on a scavenged bit of string around my neck. I was tired, but my body was strung tight like the strings of a lute, and I trembled with each step. I circled the town until I came to the tree line where the last of the children had vanished. I stood there for a moment, unsure, falling into a practiced silence. There were no footprints, and the first twinges of uncertainty begin to creep in, coloring my determination.

I closed my eyes, and that's when I heard it. A small thread of music. It wasn't so much a sound as it was a feeling. It was like a thread in my head, a vibration that when I focused on it, I could sense a small tug. I took a small step toward the origin of the music, and then another. With each step, the vibration grew, and I found myself humming along, following the trail left for me.

I don't know how far I walked—I was so focused on following the string of music by pulling myself along it that distance had no meaning. I sang to myself, and the connection between me and the revenant grew stronger. Deeper into the mountains I traveled, spotting more and more signs that a great many people had gone this way before me. Small bits of cloth and hair were caught on brambles, and the ground was stirred up by many feet.

By this point, the hum in my head had expanded to my entire body. Lightning ran through my veins, and many times I wanted to close my eyes and give in to the music entirely. It was only by repeatedly pricking my fingers on one of the points of my stakes until I drew blood that I was able to maintain my sanity.

I came eventually to a cave cut into the mountainside. Roughly the size and shape of a man, the footprints led into it. I gathered the pieces and quickly assembled a torch, desperate to reach the children before the sun sank below the mountain range and the creature was again in its element. Once I had, I used my chipped flint to light it and went to enter the passageway. I turned sideways, squeezing into it, my shoulder and hump being scraped raw by the stone. The sting of it further shook me out of the music's trance, and by the time the passageway opened up into a large cave, I was almost free of its influence entirely.

I came out into a large and shadowy cavern. A large fire burned within the damp dark, around which the missing children huddled. Their eyes were dull and glazed as they huddled together like lambs, the smoke circling up and out through a natural hole in the ceiling. They did not so much as glance up as I entered.

Several of the children had already been drained, their bodies tossed aside against the cavern walls like so much refuse. My heart wept at the sight. Their small, still corpses stood as an accusation of my inaction, as well as a testament to their parents' abandonment. I will carry that image with me until I die.

And there he was—there *it* was. On the opposite bank of the fire, lying completely prone in ragged, stained clothes, its skin even paler than before. Its eyes were closed, its body completely still while the sun held sway. My head began to throb with the silent music again as I approached. I pulled out one of my stakes, and I hovered it above the creature's chest as I knelt next to it. It did not move, but three frantic notes reverberated through me. Three words, repeating over and over again.

Put. It. Down.

My hands trembled, and I found myself struggling to put the stake against its chest.

Put. It. Down.

I tried to stab the nachzehrer, but my arms locked at the last second and the stake glanced harmlessly off the creature's ribs.

Put. It. Down.

The music in my head swelled into a crescendo, and I fought with all my might the urge to drop the stake. Sweat beaded on my forehead, and my eyes darted nervously around the room. They fell upon the dead children, and my heart constricted. I found my lips moving as I began to repeat the Lord's Prayer. My faith gave me strength, and within myself welled the will to drive the stake into the chest of the unmoving revenant.

Blood sprayed across my face, the saltiness of it stinging where my lips were chapped and raw. Without thinking, I licked my lips. Again and again, I stabbed the beast, blood spattering my hands and my pied clothing. The music stopped. When there was nothing left but a bloody pile of flesh, I stood, crying and shaking, and dragged the remains over to the waiting flames, throwing them in. They sputtered for a moment, but quickly caught fire. As it began to burn, behind me the children began to cry and scream, asking terrified questions. I knew then that its hold over them had ended, and I turned to tend to them.

In the end, some of the children chose to return to Hamelin. As we said goodbye, the eldest carrying the bodies of the children who hadn't made it, I prayed that they arrived safely and were delivered into the loving arms of their parents. For those who had become victims, I prayed for their deliverance into the arms of God and for burial in the safety of consecrated ground.

But thirty or so refused to go back to their parents, citing difficult childhoods, rampant abuse, and the stinging betrayal of being abandoned to the vampire. Despite its "death," I found myself still able to hear whispers of the nachzehrer's music—and like a hound, I could follow those threads back to wherever it had come from. Because of this, I was able to find an abandoned mountain tunnel further back in the lair—a system of caves the creature must have traversed in its hunt for blood. We did not know where else to go, or what else to do, so we decided to follow it. We who remained gathered a number of torches and went back under the mountain.

After several days of wandering the caves and following that fading music, we found an exit, squinting into the bright light. Smoke wafted across a pale sky above the treetops, and when we followed it, we came to a quiet village where another, older monastery loomed over them. We made quite an entrance—a crippled man dressed in pied clothing leading thirty children through the town square. When people approached us with nervous anger, we told them where we had come from, what had happened, and what we had done. The relief on their faces had been plain, and they quickly explained their emotions to us. It seems that years ago, the nachzehrer had taken up residence in the moldering monastery above them, preying on the people of the town below. In desperation, they had made a clumsy nighttime attack on it. They described it as a literal bloodbath, as men and women had been frozen in place by its horrible tune, and it had slaughtered them mercilessly. But in the end, it was a bitter success, and they drove the nachzehrer into the mountains.

After conferring amongst themselves, they offered us the monster's lair out of gratitude and guilt. We moved into those drafty, leaking halls, and with the help of some of the townsfolk, I built my "orphanage" of sorts. There were, of course, some delays in integration, but now, several decades on, the place is repaired and many of the children have grown and gone into town to raise their own families. They visit me often, and the other abandoned or orphaned children that I have taken in.

For the most part, my life has been well-lived. I am comfortable and loved, respected by my children and the townsfolk, despite my twisted appearance. I never gave up my colorful clothing—though the scraps are of much better quality, and they are stitched together with love and brightly colored thread.

Some nights I still wake drenched in a cold sweat, the haunting music echoing through the halls we have spent so much time painstakingly turning into a home. Occasionally, there are accusations from the townsfolk below, but they are always quick to be silenced and their fears laid to rest.

So what if my children are quicker to respond than other children, more gentle and more pliable, if only when I sing three notes in quick succession?

So what if the sun brings more pain than it used to, and so what if I have aged very little in the decades that have passed since I tasted the nachzehrer's blood?

God works in mysterious ways.

An In-Depth Tour of the Beresford Lunatic Asylum

WELCOME AND INTRODUCTION

Welcome, esteemed guests, ghosts, and the lunarly challenged, to today's private tour of the Beresford Lunatic Asylum for Lycanthropes. My name is Elsa, and I will be your tour guide for today. If you'd like to follow me, we can begin our exploration.

Operating from 1814 to 1967, Bereseford was built by the Beresfords, a British aristocratic family with skeletons and werewolves aplenty in their closet. Knowing the persecution those with lycanthropy often faced, as well as the general danger lycanthropes posed to the general public, the Beresford family commissioned the asylum in the early nineteenth century as a place where those afflicted could be safely removed from society and live in peace. It was also a place of intense study and research, with the hopes that a cure for lycanthropy could eventually be found and the residents of the adult could be reintroduced and reintegrated into polite society.

Fun fact—the term "lunatic", while often associated with mental illness, was actually first used to describe those who were affected by the moon. Any modern-day nurse will tell you about the full-moon and its effect on patients and people—haha, I can see some knowing nods in the crowd.

The multi-winged building was completed in 1813 and opened the following year under the watchful eyes of some of the most esteemed researchers and medical staff available. Beresford quickly became the preeminent European destination for those suffering from lycanthropy. Werewolves, as well as a few more exotic were-creatures, were admitted in droves. At its highest rate of incarceration, Beresford was home to over 167 'thropes of varying ages and economic backgrounds.

THE ENTRANCE

As you now know from your journey here, Beresford is located a three-hour drive from the closest major city, and the estate spans several hundred acres of the moors broken up by patches of thick forest. A thick iron gate with inlaid silver alloy also spans the entirety of the property, which was a *huge* undertaking at the time of its completion. On the off-chance one of the lycanthropes escaped, this fence penned in the escapee and allowed for them to be safely collected before they reached civilization proper.

As you drove in, you might also have noticed the fence is topped with elegantly wrought spikes, so even if a werewolf was able to endure the agonizing burning of its flesh against the inlaid silver, it would be hard-pressed to get itself over the top of the fence without severe injury. To date, silver has proven to be the best defense against lycanthropes, and Beresford incorporated it into both its landscaping and architecture to great effect.

THE GROUNDS/LANDSCAPING

When you were through the gates and bumping down the old cobblestone road, you might have noticed the dead shrubbery bordering the driveway. Those holly bushes were planted during the First World War, after a mistranslation of an old Roman text where the words *vampires* and *werewolves* were transposed. Despite its ineffectiveness as a werewolf deterrent, holly was quite a lovely bit of landscaping, and Beresford made a pretty penny every holiday season shipping in cuttings to the city as a way to further fund the research done here.

If you look further afield at the trees, you'll see they are dripping with cultivated mistletoe. Mistletoe is considered a parasitic plant that was also initially thought to be incredibly effective against werewolves. Research done here at Beresford has proven otherwise, and the mistletoe was then also shipped into the city with the holly branches.

As for the area around the asylum itself, those violet, white, and pale green flowers that you see dotting the landscape are all members of the aconitum family, more famously known as monkshood or wolfsbane. Beresford planted every variety that they could get their hands on, and they self-seeded rather extraordinarily. These plants are highly poisonous when ingested, and wolves seem to instinctively avoid them. This was the only landscaping attempt that proved fruitful for aiding in containment.

Let's go inside, shall we?

THE RECEPTION AREA

As you can see, the reception area can only be described as grand. While Beresford could technically accept werewolves from any economic status, it focused its efforts on those who could pay. It was considered a luxury estate, and many of Europe's noble families enrolled their relations at great cost. While having a werewolf or wolves plural in the family was generally considered a great shame if you were from the upper-crust, having a family member isolated at Beresford for treatment erased some of the stain affixed to the family name. For a while, it was actually seen as a marker of status.

Now, this reception area was most people's first introduction to Beresford and was the only area of the asylum open to the public. As a result, the Beresford family spared no expense in making sure it made an *impression* on the noble and wealthy families who brought their relatives here. If you look below your feet (kindly ignore the bloodstains), those rugs are hand-knitted imported Turkish rugs. The floor is quarried marble, and the large reception desk is a five hundred pound piece of mahogany teakwood bolted into the floor. Off to the side over there was a small cafe area and visiting centre, though those areas were rarely used. Visits were kept to an extreme minimum, and many abandoned their family members here and never returned.

Due to the violent nature of lycanthropy, the reception area was heavily guarded with many plainclothes and uniformed officers, both patrolling and stationed in strategic areas. All desk and office staff were trained soldiers, and every guard was outfitted with syringes of heavy sedatives, silver alloy batons, and swords. As the years passed, quick-load guns using silver bullets were also added to the required weaponry.

Just through here, please.

THE DINING ROOM

Beyond the areas that were open to the public, the rooms and wings of the asylum became increasingly utilitarian. Here we have the dining room and cafeteria, which you might find reminiscent of current high-school cafeterias. In order to prevent them from being overturned and thrown, these wooden trestle tables were handcrafted and bolted to the floor in a similar manner to the reception desk. Though they are no longer here due to the destruction of the 1967 riot, the chairs were similar. Meals were served family style and were primarily carnivorous until an outbreak of scurvy and rabbit starvation necessitated the import of fruits and vegetables to the grounds.

Now, eating in the dining room was a privilege afforded to those whose behavior was exemplary, and many guests were usually confined entirely to their rooms due to their own actions. This number increased as the years went on; the dining room was shut down entirely in 1857, and the space converted to a break room for those employed here at Beresford.

THE RECREATION ROOM

Just off the dining room, we have the recreation room. Also known as the folly of Beresford, the recreation room was only open for about eight months following the admittance of the first resident before it was permanently shuttered. It contained games, furniture, some period-appropriate exercise equipment, and a small lending library where residents could check out two books at a time to be brought back to their quarters.

Unfortunately, during the year following the opening of the asylum, management found that many of the residents were using their allotted time in the recreation room in ways that were considered inappropriate. Fights regularly broke out between frustrated residents, and if they weren't fighting, they were...attempting to reproduce or engaging in lewd acts. The library was often empty as multiple residents would try to smuggle more than their allotted allowance of reading materials back to their quarters, complaining there weren't enough books in circulation and that they were bored. Others dedicated themselves to exercise and increased rapidly in size and strength, which was deemed dangerous for the staff.

In the end, the recreation room was closed and the programs halted. The space was reallocated to an overflow wing for the infirmary.

RESIDENT QUARTERS

As we move back into the reception area, I'll have you follow me up the grand staircase to the second floor, where we will find the residential quarters. Now, your standard-sized room was twelve by eight feet and contained a bed, a desk, and a bucket. Some had the barred windows you see; others did not.

In the beginning, guests were permitted to bring in their own furniture and personalize their cells, but as the years passed, this policy was eliminated and the quarters became more uniform. This was in order to make sure there was no contraband or constructed weapons that could either be hidden in the furniture or constructed from it that would allow the residents to escape or attack the guards.

If you look along the walls here, you will see many holes and chips in the bricks from sustained gunfire. These are remnants of the 1967 riot, which I'll be happy to talk about more at the end of the tour. If you'd like to take a picture of yourselves in the cells, please feel free to do so.

There were several guests who notably got a "suite" to themselves. For example, the Marquess of Edgemont, who had considerable wealth, was allowed to inhabit three rooms due to a rather generous donation from his family following the closing of the recreation room. You could also pay more for the privilege of a windowed room.

When they were not confined to their rooms or eating in the dining hall before its closure, the residents were in the cells. If you would please follow me, we're going to go down the servant's stairs and visit the cell block on the basement level. Kindly watch your step—some of the wood is soft. We plan to replace it later this year.

THE CELLS

Spooky, aren't they? Ignoring what sounds like the rattle of chains and the lingering echoes of mournful howls, the cells were a crucial part of each guest's stay. As you can see, there were approximately two hundred of them built here into the first basement level of Beresford. Each cell is a five-foot by five-foot square space. If you look down at the stone floor, you'll notice five inlaid iron rings. Chains were affixed to these rings, and then one chain manacled to each limb. The final chain was for a leather collar that could not be reached by the hands. Each limb was kept quite taut for the duration of the incarceration.

During the days leading up to the full moon, guests were escorted down to the cells, stripped, and then either willingly or forcibly restrained. Once they were in place and the transformation had occurred, they were fed thin gruel and water through a cup attached to a long rod. If a lycanthrope attacked and broke the cup at any point, they spent the remainder of the three days without food or water as punishment.

When it came to keeping the werewolves confined, pain was the best teacher. The bars of each cell were coated with a silver-infused paint, which not only cut costs from pure silver but also helped prevent the wolves from attempting to break through the bars to either savage each other or the guards and researchers observing them. However, this was not always successful, and many werewolves and staff were injured over the years.

THE MEDICAL WING

After the full moon and following their transition back to human, guests were unclipped from their cells and brought up to the medical wing so any injuries sustained during the period of transformation and retainment could be documented and treated. Many of the residents had extended periods of time living in the medical wing as they were subject to maladies both human and lupine, and it often necessitated intense medical intervention.

You might wonder if you are hearing the echoes of agonized screams, but rest assured that any procedures done during a stay at Beresford were done entirely for the lycanthrope's benefit. While various types of anesthesia or numbing agents were experimented with, werewolves burned them off quickly because of their advanced metabolism, and many of them were awake or awoke during medical treatment.

While this might sound inhumane, please be reminded that werewolves are not considered human. The medical wing and infirmary, as well as the bordering laboratory, were the grounds for many important studies of the lycanthrope's form and anatomy. These studies are also responsible for several major scientific breakthroughs.

THE LABORATORY

When it comes to the more gruesome history of the Beresford lunatic asylum, the laboratory contains some of its darkest stories. In the pursuit of knowledge, many of the residents were subjected to various experiments. During the 1967 riot that resulted in the closure of Bereseford, the laboratories were trashed by angry lycanthropes, and most of the instruments and hard copy research were destroyed.

As for the manner of experiments and research, Beresford researchers carried out a wide variety here. They performed vivisections and autopsies on both human and lycan forms to better understand anatomy and the nature of the transformation. Weaknesses, both mythological and scientific, were rigorously tested in pursuit of better containment systems. Aconite serums were injected, organs removed, and blood filtering techniques such as dialysis were used and perfected in these rooms.

Unfortunately, as time progressed, lycanthropy became rarer in the general population, so in the interest of scientific progress many so-called "undesirable" people were also brought in and purposefully infected so that Beresford's studies could continue. During times of war or strife, government officials permitted experimentation on soldiers in order to perfect what they had hoped would be a lycan weapon, but the werewolves proved too difficult to manage during the period surrounding the full moon. They were just as likely to turn and savage their trainers as they were the enemy.

Regardless, the experiments here provided a lot of information on lycanthropy to the scientific community. The largest of these discoveries was that lycanthropy is circulated through the blood, a conclusion that was further corroborated by the next stop on today's tour: the whelping dens.

THE WHELPING DENS

We now know lycanthropy is an infectious disease passed via contact with contaminated bodily fluids, such as a bite or sexual transmission. One of the more pressing questions of the past was whether lycanthropy could also be genetically passed down, and this was the subject of multiple studies here at Beresford.

Female lycanthropes were considered quite rare in polite society, as women of the time were not usually placed in situations where lycanthropy could be transmitted. In the interest of research, the women who were admitted to Beresford were often subjected to insemination and pregnancy. Occasionally, this came as the result of a violent act by another resident, but for the most part it was through a simple and effective medical procedure. Sperm would be forcibly extracted from a male resident, which would then be inseminated into the female during her human follicular phase. While this might seem like a strange way to approach the study of lycanthropic pregnancy, when two transformed werewolves of opposite sexes were placed together, they often fought and natural copulation would not occur. Furthermore, upper management did not approve of two human-shaped werewolves engaging in sex outside the bounds of wedlock, and so insemination was the proposed solution.

If insemination resulted in a successful pregnancy, the female would be removed from the general population for further study and observation, as well as for her own protection.

Most of the time, these pregnancies ended well before the third trimester. Miscarriage was common during the monthly transformation, and the mothers rarely survived it due to acute blood loss. Despite these setbacks, some pregnancies were carried to full term, and four whelping "dens" were built in the laboratory. These were small, dark rooms with a glass wall where the pregnant werewolf could live in relative comfort and be observed at all hours of the day.

There are very few documented adolescent werewolves, as infants and children in general lack the fortitude to regularly transform without negative effects. If you have a squeamish stomach, please avert your eyes from the northeast corner of whelping den number three where, nestled in a makeshift nest of blankets, you will find the mummified remains of several pups. Two of the pups appear to have died in full lycanthropic form during the full moon. Another passed mid-transformation, and the final one achieved full reversion back to human before expiring. As for the mother, her body is not present, and we can assume that she was removed from her pups, though whether they were alive or deceased at that point is unknown.

What Bereseford learned from all of this is that while lycanthropy could be passed down genetically, they were unable to record the survival of a natural-born lycanthrope past infancy.

THE UNDERGROUND TUNNELS

Going deeper down into the heart of Beresford, we come to the underground tunnel system. Watch your step when walking through the hallways—they are very damp and you can easily slip. If you do slip, please remember that you signed a waiver at the beginning of the tour absolving us of all responsibility for any and all potential physical harm. Yes, that means you can't sue.

Used primarily to move supplies, bodies, and illicit materials, these service tunnels were original to the building. They were further expanded during the period following the First World War. Each of these branching corridors leads back up to the ground and cell floors. All rooms barring the residential quarters had close access to underground service hallways, and for those on the second and third floors there were many hidden "servants" staircases so these tunnels could be accessed out of sight of the residents.

These tunnels were not generally known to the residents of Beresford, and thus were instrumental in the escape of surviving staff during the 1967 riot. The few staff members that did manage to survive the riot used these tunnels to escape the general slaughter. While the tunnels do extend for many kilometers, we're going to exit here, out into the cemetery.

THE CEMETERY

We're going to end our tour here, at the cemetery, where over three thousand lycanthropes are estimated to have been buried during Beresford's years of operation. You'll notice that there are only about two hundred gravestones—those belong to various staff that died on the premises. Due to the infectious nature of lycanthropy and general superstition, any staff mauled or eaten were required by law to be buried on the grounds. The lycanthropes, however, were buried in paupers' graves without markers or ceremony, and it is only through the use of ground-penetrating radar that we've been able to find any remains at all.

It only seems fitting to also talk about the ending of the Beresford Lunatic Asylum here at the cemetery. On April 4th, 1967, an incident occurred that would shut down Beresford for good. While there were several attempted escapes or attacks a year, this riot was by far the bloodiest and most violent to occur in the history of the grounds.

That afternoon, a guard by the name of Nathanial Boone was escorting a particularly problematic resident to the laboratory for a scheduled appointment when the human-shaped lycanthrope found itself subject to the change outside of the full moon, which was a completely undocumented phenomenon at the time.

There have been many theories about why this might have occurred. It could have been an intense bout of fear triggering a survival tactic, a result of one of the many serums injected or experiments performed, lunar reflections on the ocean or a misplaced sense of internal time, but despite many discussions about this abnormal occurrence, there has never been a truly satisfactory explanation put forth.

Upon transforming, the resident, whose name has been lost to history, violently attacked Mr. Boone and killed him, In an intense sign of mental fortitude not previously expected of lycanthropes, the resident then showed enough intelligence to retrieve the keys from the guard before opening up all the doors to the residents' quarters, releasing over 140 werewolves into the halls of Beresford at once.

Furthermore, the inexplicable transformation of the original resident seemingly triggered a domino effect, and the other werewolves began to transform as well. While not all the residents morphed into their lycan form, many of them did. Despite the use of bullets and batons, the guards and scientists were quickly overwhelmed and consequently slaughtered.

Most of the staff died that evening. When a few workers escaped through the tunnels and raised the alarm, the military responded and set up a perimeter outside the gates. However, no lycanthropes were ever observed in the weeks that followed, and the bodies of the researchers and werewolves that died in the riot were never collected.

The few employees who did escape never truly left, as they were so traumatized by the violence that several of them committed suicide in the following years. Upper management had been completely decimated by the riot, and none of the other noble families were willing to step in and take over the running of the asylum. Beresford was abandoned, and the property fell into disrepair. After many years with no sightings, the property was reopened for tours such as this one.

Ah, I see we have a question. Yes, sir, the one with the hat.

Sorry, I can't hear you. Oh, what happened to the werewolves following the 1967 emergency closure of Beresford?

There are a lot of different theories. Some believe the transformation outside of the lunar cycle drained them of their "life force" and they died. Some people assume they tried to escape, but the many barriers, such as the growing aconite or silver fence, killed them before they ever reached the gates.

The truth is something entirely different. While many of the lycanthropic residents did die during the riot, the rest remained here. They formed a pack, which has continued to grow, safe within the silver boundary of the grounds. They built houses within the hundreds of acres and formed a close-knit community.

After the establishment of the internet, the pack found other lycanthropes online and began recruiting, many of them moving to the grounds and seeking safety and comfort in numbers. Thanks to the progress made within the walls of Beresford during its years of operation, the werewolves have used the scientific knowledge gleaned here to successfully breed, birth, and raise a new generation of lycanthropes. In fact, a full third of the current pack was born on the grounds.

And now they give private tours, established solely through word of mouth and attended by only the very brave or the very stupid. Sometimes they pluck new members from the tour groups, those they think would be best suited for life as a lycanthrope. Other groups go home perfectly fine, their morbid curiosity sated. Other tours...end a little more messily.

Ah, here they come now. As you can see, the lycanthropes of the Beresford Lunatic Asylum are thriving. See how thick their pelts have grown, how strong and muscular they have become, and how they can transform in the light of day so far from a full moon! Look at those slavering jaws and intelligent eyes. Beautiful, aren't they?

They know, so much more than any of you, what exactly humans are capable of. They are more than willing to take their pound of flesh and put it on the dinner table as penance for all the lycanthropes suffered at your hands for over 150 years.

Now, if you'll excuse us, our families are hungry.

THAT DARK AND ENDLESS SHORE

THERE IS A point in most people's lives when a certain event bisects it—there is the time *before*, and the time *after*. For some, this event is a happy one, perhaps even a blessed one; the birth of a baby, a new marriage, a promotion. For others, the line is a dark one that casts a permanent shadow on everything that is cursed enough to follow it. For me, that event occurred on Halloween when I was twelve years old, in a small suburb of the city where I grew up.

Lincoln had the idea of filling the small haunted maze in front of 54 Colborne with rotten eggs. It began as a petty revenge plot. Lincoln lived just off of Colborne on East River Street and was considered the absolute terror of the neighborhood. He regaled us for weeks about how the old man who lived at Colborne was constructing a Halloween maze on the front lawn out of painted plywood and Dollar Store decorations. Mr. Robinson, for that was the old man's name, yelled at him several times in the past over various harmless jokes and pranks—such as Lincoln playing ding-dong-ditch or leaving a carefully curated bag of flaming dog poop, harvested from Lincoln's backyard courtesy of his stepmom's little Yorkshire terrier. Mr. Robinson had a chat with Lincoln's parents, and after being grounded and restricted access to his brand-new Nintendo, Lincoln declared war. He

wanted to pull off a prank that would ruin Mr. Robinson's reputation and all the hours the old man had spent on his front lawn constructing his ramshackle maze.

However, a twelve-year-old cannot generally be considered a criminal mastermind. Lincoln settled on what was essentially a twist on the tradition of egging the house on All Hallow's Eve. The six of us—Lincoln, Rob, Henry, Kevin, Jennifer, and I—were each given the task of collecting several eggs from our parents' refrigerators and having them ripen unrefrigerated over the course of several weeks.

"It has to be somewhere warm," he reminded us as we huddled on the school playground, plotting his revenge for what I now realize were perfectly reasonable responses to Lincoln's budding delinquency. He ran a freckled hand through his shock of red hair as he spoke, scrunching up his nose. "When it's Halloween, we'll meet up with the eggs in our candy bags. We'll go into the maze and smash the eggs inside. That'll show him for blabbing to Linda about me."

It didn't cross his mind that we would also be subject to the cloud of stench that would happen when we inevitably smashed the eggs and gassed the maze, and we'd be trapped inside with it. To be fair, it didn't cross any of our minds. Again, twelve-year-olds aren't usually considered masterminds.

On Halloween night at the appointed time, we met at Lincoln's house. He answered the door dressed in white face makeup and a cut-up sheet. I was tall and gangly at that age, all stretched out limbs and bony joints, and so I dressed up as the scarecrow from Wizard of Oz. The straw I had shoved in my collar itched, and I couldn't stop scratching at my neck. Kevin, who was short and rather round, had decided to match me by dressing up as the cowardly lion. Jenny dressed as a modest Madonna, and Rob wore only a jester's hat. He was too cool for a full costume, but he couldn't pass up the opportunity to lord his position as "class clown" over us.

We stood on the front lawn, shifting nervously as the trick-or-treaters first trickled, and then flooded, down the street. Everywhere you looked there were jack-o'-lanterns, plastic sheet ghosts hanging from trees, groups of parents milling around and drinking surreptitiously from their thermoses of "coffee".

"Does everyone have their eggs?" Lincoln demanded.

We all nodded, except for Jenny. In hindsight, I bet she had never planned on actually joining us on the war trail. She probably hadn't even snuck any eggs.

"You can have some of mine," Rob offered, a blush covering his dark cheeks. He was more than a little sweet on Jenny. She gave him a reluctant smile, and the tips of his ears turned red.

Henry grinned at me nervously, his large front teeth featuring prominently in his round and freckled face. "Should we do some trick-or-treating first?"

"We're a little old for that," Kevin argued.

I raised my pillowcase. It had the eggs, carefully packaged, already in the bottom. "I could go for some candy."

"Me too," Jenny said.

"I suppose we should," Lincoln begrudgingly agreed. "Makes it seem less suspicious when we go in."

We made our way up the street, running across lawns, dead leaves crunching underfoot as we dodged the roving packs of younger children as we went door-to-door and collected our goods. It was a dry, cool night, perfect for Halloween festivities. The sun had already set, and the shadows of the streetlamps reminded me of long, bony fingers reaching out to grab at us, sending a chill down my spine.

We turned right onto Colborne Street. The place was bustling and loud—every single house was decorated, and some people had clearly driven in from other neighbourhoods. Only a few houses down from the street junction, we could see number 54. The entire front lawn had been transformed and a crowd had formed out front. We skipped the houses next to it, drawn to it as moths to a flame.

There stood a lopsided structure where before there had been only dry, yellowing grass. Now, large sheets of black-painted plywood, the paint already flaking and peeling, had been hammered together into a crude building. You could get away with Halloween displays like that back then, when people didn't care so much about safety or eye-sores. Homemade signs were jammed roughly into the inch of grass between the structure and the sidewalk. A single, sad-looking string of orange-coloured Christmas lights hung around the entrance to the maze. Out in front of it, literally on the pavement, sat an old man in a weathered blue and white checkered chair.

Mr. Robinson.

He was mostly bald, with a few wispy white tufts of hair that stuck out from his liver-spotted scalp like small clouds of cotton candy. He raised his head at us as we approached. He was heavily wrinkled, his back bent and twisted, hunched over an old, chipped bowl that sat in his lap. He reminded me of a withered old apple that had rolled under the couch and been forgotten.

There was a small line of younger children in front of us, and with every "trick or treat!" he would drop a single, sad-looking candy into the proffered pillowcase or bucket. Others would walk past him into the maze, tittering nervously. We waited our turn, and as we came up to him, his eyes narrowed.

"Hello Lincoln," he said.

"Hi, Mr. Robinson," Lincoln said, the very picture of a contrite and humbled child. The two of them stared at each other for a moment, a silent standoff that made the rest of us uncomfortable.

"What'll it be, boys?" Mr. Robinson said after a hostile minute. "And lady, it appears," he said with a nod of his head to the nervous Jenny. She gave him a small and anxious wave. "Will it be a trick?" He gestured to the dilapidated-looking maze behind him. A pair of gnarled, arthritic fingers pinched a generic red sucker from the bowl on his lap and dangled it towards us. "Or treat?"

"Treat," Jennifer said hurriedly. I saw Lincoln give her a quick kick against her half-tied sneaker. She stared at the ground as Mr. Robinson dropped the sucker into her bucket.

"Trick," Lincoln said loudly. "I want a trick."

"Me too," Kevin said with a mean, lop-sided grin. He radiated anticipatory smugness, and I felt the urge to hit him.

"I want the maze," Rob said.

"What about you two boys?" Mr. Robinson said, looking at Henry and me. Something in his eyes caught me off-guard and made me uneasy.

"I think I'll have a treat," Henry stammered out eventually. Jennifer shot him a grateful smile. Lincoln rolled his eyes and turned to glare at me.

"What do you want to do, Elias?"

I looked between him and Mr. Robinson. "Trick, I think." A strange, irrational fear pooled in my stomach. "I think I want a trick."

"Well, get on with it then," Mr. Robinson said, an ominous twinkle in his eye. "Try out the maze. See how you like it."

Henry and Jennifer stepped off to the side. The four of us shuffled forward, Lincoln glaring daggers the entire time at the two Benedict Arnolds who carefully avoided meeting his gaze. Henry ripped the wrapper off of his sucker with a loud crinkle and jammed into his mouth.

"We'll wait here," he muttered.

The entrance to the maze was a tattered old purple curtain set against the black-painted walls. Around it were crudely spray-painted in red phrases like "Turn back!" and "NO ESCAPE!" The top of the maze was also closed off, a roof constructed of assorted materials haphazardly nailed into place, overlapping one another in a ramshackle manner. Lincoln strolled in, yanking the curtain to the side so violently that I winced, surprised he didn't rip the whole thing down. The other two boys followed, swaggering in. I hesitated.

"Go on, then," Mr. Robinson said, and made a shooing motion. "Have fun!" He grinned at me then, his smile short an awful lot of teeth.

I entered the door. The small room at the entrance to the maze was cramped—the four of us were crowded together shoulder to shoulder. Two separate turns headed off deeper into the maze. Around us, fake cobwebs dripped down from the ceiling where they had been hastily stapled, tickling our noses.

"Okay, Rob, you and Elias go that way, and me and Kevin will go this way," he ordered. "Split up after the first turnoff and plant the eggs. Stomp on them if you have to—make the whole place reek. This isn't a large maze so we should be able to cover everything in stink. We'll all meet out front." He and Kevin went forward without another word, leaving Rob and me hunched in the front room.

"Let's go," Rob said. "I want to keep trick-or-treating."

I hesitated. He nudged me. "Don't chicken out now. He'll kill you, dude," he reminded me.

I nodded mutely and followed him, unable to shake the feeling that what we were about to do was a terrible mistake. It was only a few more feet into the maze until our path diverged. Rob went down the left, and I went to the right, creeping through the tunnel. I found a dead end and dug through my candy bag to the half-carton of eggs, carefully cut with scissors and wrapped in one of my mother's bright yellow dish-towels. It was my contribution to the prank—three eggs that I had hidden in our heated garage right by the vent. I looked at their smooth white surfaces and picked one out to hold in my hand. It sat there in my palm, nowhere near as heavy as my conscience told me it was. I went to place it down and stomp on it, but something stopped me. I looked at the remaining two eggs, closed the carton, and buried it back within the bags of chips and chocolate bars. I didn't bother to smash the egg I left out. I carefully placed it in a corner of the dead end and left it there. I didn't want to tell the boys that I had entirely chickened out and tripped while crossing the finish line.

The eyes of the plastic skulls watched me as I turned around. I kicked a fake bone out of the way, and when I turned to where I thought I had come from, there sat a dead end. Convinced I must have gotten mixed up, I went in the other direction. I walked for two minutes down the hall before I got confused. Even more so when I whirled around and found several more offshoots that hadn't been there before. I followed one of them, my heart beginning to thud in my chest. I was lost—but how could that be? How could I get lost in a maze that spanned the front yard of one old man? When I got out, I would never hear the end of it.

I sped up, first speed-walking, then jogging, then full-out running. I turned this way and that, but no matter what I did, I couldn't find the exit. It made no sense. More and more paths continued to open up ahead of me and behind me.

I stopped, straining for any sound. In the distance, I could make out shouting and recognized it as Rob. He called my name, over and over. The edge of panic in his voice made me wonder if he was as lost as I was. As I tried to follow it, the shouts and screams of Kevin and Lincoln faded in and out, too. I ran and I ran and I ran, calling back at them, but one by one they went quiet. Their silence was more terrifying than their screaming.

"Rob?! Kevin? Are you there?! Where are you!" I shrieked until my voice was hoarse. Only silence answered me. I couldn't hear anything—not the laughter of the other children as they wandered up and down Colborne Street, nor the chattering of parents, nor even the sound of the wind. My ears strained for even a hint of the campy music playing from the nearby boombox placed on a festive porch, but there was nothing. I kept running, cheap skulls badly glued to the corners of intersecting walls leering down at me as I followed the darkly painted paths. Panic spurred me on, and I banged my shoulders against the walls as I careened wildly down the turns without a thought to where I was going, driven only by the need to *get out, get out, get out*. At some point I dropped my pillowcase, abandoning it in those empty halls.

I don't know how long I ran through the maze, but when my lungs began to burn and my legs trembled, I stopped for a moment to catch my terrified breath. Once I had caught it, I shoved at the boards, pushing against them with my weight. Tears leaked from the corners of my eyes.

"Let me out!" I screamed. "Let me out! Please, someone, anyone!"

In desperation, I slammed my whole body against the boards, again and again. Finally, I felt some give, and I threw myself at the wall with everything I had, hoping it would fall, triggering a domino effect that would release me back onto Colborne Street. My costume tore on the cheap wood, splinters snatching and ripping at it. My shoulder was bruised and aching by the time the wall finally collapsed outwards, taking me with it. I fell onto the ground, and then everything stopped making the little sense it already had.

I landed on thick, grimy grey sand. It wasn't dry, but that didn't stop it from being soft, and I sank into it as if it were an old mattress. My mouth had been open when I fell, and it quickly filled. The sand had an almost viscous quality to it, and when I tried to spit it out, I was only mildly successful. The grit lodged in my teeth and carpeted my tongue. It dried out my mouth, and for several minutes I gagged and pawed at my face. It tasted the way bread mold smells, and several times I had to stop myself from vomiting.

After I had finally gotten most of the sand out of my mouth, I raised my head and took in my surroundings. I was in the middle of a beach that stretched on in an eerily straight line for what seemed like forever in both directions. Behind me, in the direction I had fallen from, was the same grey sand extending as far as the eye could see, a dismal desert devoid of any sign of life. Directly ahead of me was an ocean, though it was unlike any ocean I had ever seen before, in person or in pictures.

The water was so dark as to be black. It thrashed around, the whitecaps a deep and dingy grey on top of the inky waves. There were no islands, no rocky outcrops; the water went on and on until it merged with the sky. Above it, a dark sky roiled, clouds tumbling over one another, speeding towards me and then away as if someone had pressed fast-forward on a VHS tape. I felt nauseous just looking at it—the way it moved while I stood still was disorienting and threw me off-kilter. It reminded me of the time I'd secretly sipped at my father's whiskey until I was dizzy, grimacing at the burn of it as it slid down my throat.

"Hello? Is anybody here?" I called. The air seemed to steal my very words—they were muffled and blurred. It sounded as if I were talking to myself from a great distance.

Despite everything, the roiling of the clouds, the whitecaps of that black ocean, the air was still. There wasn't so much as a breeze to ruffle my hair. It was as if I alone stood in the eye of some unknown storm, unaffected by what had to be hurricane-level winds that blew around me. The air was cold but humid, and I immediately felt damp.

There was no plywood underneath me, I realized. It was as if I had pushed my way into another world. I stood up, my boots sinking into the sand. It sucked at my feet like mud, and it was not without some effort that I made my way down to the shore to stare at the waves. By that point, I was outright weeping, beyond the point of mere terror. I was in another world, alone. I wanted my friends, I wanted my Halloween back, I wanted to finish up trick-or-treating, and more than anything in the world, I wanted my mother.

I don't know how long I stood there crying while the waves crashed and the sky boiled. I don't even know when I took my first step, picking a random direction and beginning to follow the shoreline. I walked for hours.

Maybe days. Nothing ever changed—I didn't grow hungry, or thirsty, or tired. I never had to go to the bathroom. I struggled step after step, trying not to get bogged down in the shifting sand. Above me, the sky continued to simmer, and the ocean continued to slap monotonously against the shore. The stink of the ocean and rotting seaweed was constant, and soon my tears were nothing but salt trickling down my chapped cheeks. I was a ghost, trapped on a strange world, haunting a shore that never changed for what was both an eternity and a blink of the eye.

It was in the hundredth hour or on the hundredth day that something finally changed. As I trudged along, my feet and heart numb, there was a blur on the horizon. I squinted at it, feeling something for the first time in what seemed like a long time. It was not hope or despair, but a mild curiosity that penetrated my existence. I did not change my pace, but trekked steadily towards it as the object came into clearer focus.

It was a body. A humanoid figure, half-in and half-out of the black surf. It was face down in the sand, its skin grey and clammy. Its arms and legs were long, with large, paddle-like feet. Long, webbed fingers with sharp claws dug into the sand, as if it had pulled itself torturously from the water.

I crouched beside it and reached out a hand to touch it. It was cold— ice cold, and it had roughly the same texture as tapioca. I shoved the body with some effort to roll it over, and I pulled back, a soundless cry escaping from my lips.

Its head was oversized and vaguely shaped like some sort of cephalopod. Taking up a full half of its face were two giant eyes, pitch-black, staring sightlessly up at the turbulent sky. Its wide and grotesque mouth was open as if in a scream, and long, needle-like teeth jutted from its mouth like an anglerfish. On either side of that gaping void were two lengthy tentacles that reminded me of a squid's—with a wide, fleshy end. It was covered not in suckers, but with small, fishhook-like spines. I could picture those appendages grabbing me, those hooks sinking into my tender flesh and pulling me in towards that massive mouth as we floated in the pitch-black of the ocean. I closed my eyes and gave a little whimper before steeling myself and continuing to examine it.

It seemed as if it had partially melted, its form sagged into the sand. I wondered if its bones were more like cartilage than traditional skeletal anatomy. I shifted closer, both terrified of and desperate for this strange change in scenery. I was right next to it, staring at those horrible teeth, when it moved.

One of those webbed hands reached out and feebly grabbed at my legs. Its long nails still managed to scratch my ankle. The white-hot pain of it, the dripping of the blood down my ankle, was the most physical sensation I had felt since I'd arrived, and I was almost grateful for it. I fell back and landed hard, began scrambling backwards as it opened and closed its mouth. Gills I had not noticed previously fluttered along its ribs, and it made a terrible rasping noise as it tried to turn itself back over. It succeeded, and its squid-like eyes fixed on me as it made another pathetic effort to pull itself towards me, teeth snapping weakly.

I pulled myself up and turned to run. My foot caught on the sand. I tripped, arms pinwheeling for balance as my brain screamed at me. I went sprawling, but instead of sinking into the damp sand, I fell against solid ground, my chin jamming up into my skull as my teeth chomped down on my tongue. My mouth filled with blood.

Only when I dizzily sat up did I realize I was back in the maze. I froze. I could hear the laughter of the other children, the creak of the wind against the plywood. The walls were nowhere near as firm as they had been, and they wobbled in the wind as I stood up, mute with shock.

I heard the laughter; a young girl ran past me deeper into the maze, her dark hair fanning out behind her. The sight of another human being had my eyes filling with tears, and I staggered in the direction that she had come from. Within seconds, that familiar purple curtain appeared, and I threw myself through it without a second thought, landing heavily on my knees. Rob was already there, his eyes shadowed as he cradled his arm. He did not offer to help me up, only stared back into the maze. Off to the side, Jennifer and Henry stood there, gaping at my dramatic appearance.

A moment later, Lincoln stumbled out, staggered towards a bush, and threw up into it. Kevin came last, limping slightly, face empty of all emotion.

"Whoa there, boys," Mr. Robinson said, drawing our attention. He still sat in his fold-out chair. "Something go rotten in there? Get a little too scared?"

He turned to me and smiled, a smile that brimmed with both malice and delight. "How did you like your trick?" he asked. "Was it a good one?"

Lincoln stared at him mutely, and Rob began to weep softly. Kevin just turned around and began walking away, his face blank. Henry and Jenny looked at each other with confusion in their eyes. Henry had the sucker stick still poking out from the corner of his mouth, and he rolled it around as he opened his mouth to say something to us, but he thought better of it and closed it.

That heavy moment was broken when a new gaggle of children ran up, their sweet voices all chorusing in unison as they clambered for a treat. One of the small boys, dressed as Ghostbuster, broke away from the group and ran into the maze.

"Don't! It's a trap!" I said hoarsely, reaching out after him. The boy's mother, dressed as a ladybug with a red tulle skirt, glanced at me with confusion before turning back to Mr. Robinson. The young boy disappeared from sight as he headed deeper into the maze, his laughter echoing back out at us. If I hadn't been so terrified, I would have run back in to grab him myself.

"Sorry, Greg," she said to the old man. "He hasn't stopped talking about the maze all night, so we wanted to come back and do it again."

Mr. Robinson laughed, a wheezing noise that sent the hairs on the back of my neck rising. "I'm glad he enjoyed it so much. He can run it as many times as he'd like." The little Ghostbuster popped out of another, smaller exit that I had noticed before.

"Again!" he said gleefully. "One more time!"

"What about you, boys?" Mr. Robinson said, his blue and watery eyes roving over us before finally snagging on Lincoln. In his voice was a meanness that I had never heard from an adult, and haven't since. "Do you want to go another round?"

None of us ever spoke of what we experienced that night. I don't know if the others ended up on the same desolate beach that I did, if they were sent elsewhere, or if they were just trapped in that terrible, never-ending maze.

My scratches turned to scars. The group slowly fell apart. Lincoln withdrew entirely from his role as our de facto leader and as our friend. Jennifer drifted away to join a group of girls. Henry became a nerd, hanging out with the kids who spent their Friday nights studying. Kevin became a goody-two shoes, but not in an endearing way. He became a brown-noser, a sniveling suck-up who tried to integrate himself with every adult, his eyes always haunted. I hear he sells insurance now. Rob withdrew into himself and prefers his own company to the company of others. Two years later, I moved away to the South, and I never spoke to any of the others again.

I looked up Mr. Robinson many years later, once the internet had become a thing. He died ten years after that Halloween at the ripe old age of ninety-seven. He was survived by his two daughters, one of whom moved into his house and continued his now-famous tradition of the Halloween maze.

I still dream about that night, about that dark and endless shore and rolling sky, while the stink of brine and rotting seaweed fills my nostrils and my mouth until it gags me. The sand threatens to pull me down, and I struggle towards two dim shapes at the edge of the water. One of them raises a blurry hand and motions me closer. When I reach them, that thing is still lying in the sand, half in and out of the black water. Its tentacles have disintegrated into a translucent jelly, and its face has rotted and has half slid off the cartilage underneath. Horrible giant eye sockets stare at me, and a small black crab crawls out of one and scuttles my way.

Mr. Robinson stands there over the corpse, hands shoved deep in his pockets, his eyes bright with unrestrained glee. Its puckered mouth moves, and the words are sucked away by that oppressive air. That doesn't stop me from knowing what he's saying, his lips moving in such exaggerated movements that I can't avoid reading them.

"Trick," he says, the word filling me with a horrible dread. "Trick."

Red in Tooth and Claw

THE VILLAGE SQUARE was empty of people, except for the remnants of ghosts; red stains that had seeped in between the weathered stones, sinking down into the dusty earth. A few broken wooden tables, overturned and with splintered tops, littered the outskirts of the square. Where it was bare, the earth was chewed up and ragged from a great many panicked feet. A bitter wind blew, causing the buildings to raise a mournful howl as it tore at and through them. The windows facing the square were shuttered and bolted, and the oppressive sky was as grey and leached of colour as the rest of the town. The air was heavy, a weighted blanket that threatened to press Father Wilhelm Bauer into the now-tainted ground.

He stood at the edge of the road that led into the center of the small town, steeling himself with a silent prayer. Taking a deep breath, he crossed it, his footsteps ringing out and echoing through it as he crossed the square and headed down a small side road, towards the building that now served as a makeshift prison. Behind him, Karl followed silently, his hand gripping the worn handle of his axe, eyes skipping and catching on every red splatter that painted the portrait of an afternoon gone horribly wrong.

They didn't bother to knock when they arrived at the solid wood door that marked their destination. It opened with a screech, and the five men

who stood in the front room turned towards them. Their faces were long and pale, and more than one of them bore red-rimmed eyes and blotchy faces.

"She's in the cellar, chained," one said, stepping forward and running a hand through his thick brown hair. "It is unlike anything I have ever seen. It is a demon, Father, that has done this."

Father Bauer took the man's cold, chapped hands into his own. "It will be alright," he said, but the man only pulled back.

"Through that door," the man said, jerking his head towards the far wall before he turned his back on the priest. The other four men did not say a thing, only averted their eyes. "May the grace of God go with you."

"He is always with me," Father Bauer murmured. Behind him, he could hear Karl shifting as he removed his axe from where it hung from his belt, hefting it in his hands. The door protested as he opened it, revealing a set of worn stairs that descended into the dark. At the bottom of the stairs, a candle flickered, casting shadows up the walls.

Father Bauer went down the narrow, claustrophobic passage, Karl following close behind him. The stairs groaned underfoot. At the bottom, there was a small table where light wavered from several new candles set into holders. They were so new that the long, smooth pillars reminded him of bones, and he couldn't stop himself from making a noise deep in his throat. Something rustled in the dark in response, and when he came to the bottom of the staircase, he took a moment to take in his new surroundings.

The cellar was small—there was enough space for several men to stand comfortably, but not much more. Karl stayed on the bottommost stair to conserve space, his shoulders hunched as his head brushed the low ceiling. An assortment of boxes and casks had been shoved off to one side, and in the corner opposite from the haphazard piles, someone stood in the dim, fitted with battered and scratched-up manacles around their hands and feet, and thick chains were attached to the restraint, looping around and around them and tied to several different objects. The person standing there was barely able to move from how tightly the chains were drawn. Around their neck was a rope as thick as a child's forearm, tied in a noose that connected around an old cask. In the low light, the priest could see that their neck was rubbed raw and oozing.

The eyes of the prisoner and the priest met, and Bauer could not hold back his surprised gasp.

"Malina," he said. "You?"

Malina grinned. Her mouth was stained red. Between her crooked teeth, bits of ragged colourless flesh were trapped and fluttered with each of her labored breaths. She was drenched in dried blood. It clung to her skin, peeling away here and there and littering the ground like gruesome snowflakes around her bare and filthy feet. Her dress was stiff with it, and her hair hung in lanky coils to her waist. Darkness crowded around her, shadows rippling across her skin as if they were alive. Her eyes glinted like an animal's in the depths of night. They glowed from the corner, and he felt the hair along the back of his neck and his arms rise in alarm.

"Father," she said, her voice polite. "How lovely to see you."

The scent of death rolled over Father Bauer then, the tang of iron and meat, and he had to stop himself from gagging. Karl took a deep breath in behind him. With a rattle of chains, she tried moving further into the light before being yanked back with a choking rasp. Her eyes narrowed as she peered behind Father Bauer.

"And Karl," she said with delight. "Come to hit me again? You ruined my fun with that axe of yours." She reached up to tenderly touch the large goose egg and traced with delicate fingers the dark bruise that dripped down her forehead. "Though," she said after a moment, with a leer and a wink, "we could always have a different bit of fun down on the ground."

Karl was silent. She tilted her head at his lack of acknowledgement and turned her attention back to the priest.

"Come to bless me, Father? Pray over me? Perhaps even give me last rites?" Her voice was strong and confident. "What if I told you I didn't want them?"

"Malina," Father Bauer whispered. "What has happened to you?"

"Nothing bad," she said. "Nothing bad at all."

"You were in the pews not four days ago," he said. "I watched you count your beads. We announced your engagement." Her blonde head had bowed, a small smile playing across her lips as those around her had whispered their congratulations.

She snorted then. "Yes. Good little Malina, the perfect daughter, perfect friend and soon to be the perfect wife. So restrained and careful, and so absolutely bursting with urges pressed so far down that they may as well have not existed."

"You killed those people. Why would you want to kill all those people?"

"Why does anyone do anything? I was hungry, so I ate."

"Five people are dead, more wounded," Father Bauer said, making the sign of the cross. "You were never like this. Something must have happened to you. A demon, a devil. How did you—" he choked then, the memories of the carnage he'd seen as he had been called out to the square earlier that afternoon to tend to the dead and dying following the massacre. He never would have thought Malina capable.

"Come a little closer, Father. I'll give you my full confession."

He took a step closer, and her fingers curled and her lips pulled back into a snarl and she lunged for him. The chains stopped her, and the rope strangled her, and he scrambled back, just out of reach as she tried to pull the rope off.

"Can't blame a girl for trying," she said with a sneer as he caught his breath, his pulse pounding. Behind him, Karl crouched, his axe in hand, every line in his body tense and ready. "But fine. I'll tell you." She pitched her voice lower. This time he did not bother to get closer.

"I didn't think myself capable either," she said. "But then I met something in the woods." Her small pink tongue darted out to lick at her lips. "I met *someone* in the woods," she said. "And they knew, they knew about all the different longings I had held suppressed for so long, the kinds of violence that I craved. They told me it would be okay to let it all out, that I should, and so I took their advice."

"You met the devil," Father Bauer whispered, crossing himself. "You met Satan himself." In his mind's eye, flames licked at the bodies of the damned, their cries echoing throughout his head. Malina was there, writhing and screaming.

"Don't bring your God or your Devil into this," she spat at him with such venom that he recoiled. "I met *myself* along the road. It was me, from my pretty red hair down to my littlest toe. She told me I didn't have to hide anymore—that *we* didn't have to hide anymore. That in my deepest of hearts I am an animal, and to be an animal is to be free."

She leaned as far as the chains would allow. "Do you know what it's like to strain against something, Father? To fight your baser instincts with every thread of your being?" She grinned at him. "I bet you do."

The image of the young widow Koch flew to his mind unbidden. She was three decades younger than him, and still deep in her grief. He thought of the long nights where she had sat with him in his room as they prayed together, mourning her young husband and seeking the light of the Lord. He thought of her white hands and pink cheeks, the way her flaxen hair had gleamed in the candlelight, the way it made his sinful desire strain painfully against his robes.

"There you go, Father," Malina cooed. "That's right."

He crossed himself and shook himself free of her influence. "You made a deal with a devil. Tell me about it."

"There was no devil, old man. It was me there this morning, on the road to my grandmother's house, as clearly as I would see myself in a mirror," she replied. "And I was terrifying and glorious. I was scared at first and asked who she was. 'I am you,' she said to me. 'But your eyes are so much bigger than mine,' I said, and they were. They were so big, Father, that I could not stop myself from falling into them. 'All the better to see beneath your skin and know you, my dear,' she told me."

Malina paused for a moment.

"I felt seen, Father—for the first time in my pathetic life, I felt *seen*. In that moment, I was exposed, a skeleton unearthed, breathing fresh air after being buried for so long. I cannot tell you the wonderful fear I felt at that moment. And then I said to myself, 'What big ears you have.' She told me, 'All the better to hear the whispers of your wanton heart.' She winked at me then, and I could feel myself relaxing. We were becoming friends, she and I. Finally, I said to her, 'What big teeth you have.' She smiled then, and her mouth was full of fangs. 'All the better to rend and tear.' I wasn't afraid anymore. I wanted to use those teeth just as she would. In fact, I did, and they worked wonderfully." Malina looked past the priest to the hunter still standing on the stairs. "Wouldn't you agree, Karl?"

Karl was silent, and she shifted in her chains.

"What happened then?" Father Bauer urged.

Malina tried to cross her arms, but failed. "She jumped at me then, but when she made contact, she was gone, and I was all alone in those deep, dark woods."

"You are a demon," Father Bauer said. "A demon that has entered Malina. Turned her from the quiet kind soul that she was into a murderer."

"*I am Malina*," she laughed. "You just don't understand. You all think women are just vicious of tongue, but did you ever stop to think that we are just as wild as the rest of you men? That perhaps we have the same dark urges that run through your veins and your bodies? That beneath our soft and supple skin, we hide our inner wolves and force ourselves not to howl at the moon? We force ourselves into our human guises, forgetting what it means to be wild."

Father Bauer found his lips moving. Prayers spilled forth from them, frantic and afraid. They had no effect on Malina; she continued with dark glee.

"You think the favor of your God keeps you safe from your animal instincts?" She gyrated against the air and laughed as he shrunk back further. "You think someone will come along and save you from yourselves? You're children, crying in the dark, afraid of your own shadow. I just let mine in."

"Leave the girl," he said to the thing wearing Malina's shape. "Leave her be. In the name of the Father and of the Son and of the Holy Spirit, be gone from this place."

"I am the girl," she said with a hiss. "What do you not understand? Even now, you can't even comprehend the idea that this is who I am, who I was meant to be. That the only reason that I killed those people, embraced myself, is because something else did it. I am me, I have always been me."

Karl spoke for the first time, his deep voice resolute. "She needs to die, Father."

"There's our strong woodsman," she purred. "See? There's a man who follows his instincts. He hunts, he kills, he is everything I am and more. He is brimming with violence and hunger. He knows what it means to let it out." She turned back to the priest. "You want me dead. You'll want to torture a confession out of me, even though I give it willingly. Once you feel like I have been punished enough and I have repented, you'll burn me just like all the other so-called witches. Granted, my crimes were a bit more...juicy than theirs." She grinned at that and licked her lips.

"We will rid our town of you," Karl rumbled. "We have no place for demons here."

"Oh, you'll never be rid of me," Malina said airily. "You know what I am. I'm here, and I will always be here. You think that death can stop me? Do you think that something as old and as cruel as your own inner nature is something that can be restrained forever?" She leaned towards them again, bubbling laughter spilling over her lips.

Karl moved then, his body coiled and angry. He pushed roughly past the priest, knocking him into the wall. Father Bauer fell against it, sliding to the ground, stunned and horrified, unable to tear his eyes away from Malina's piercing gaze that pinned him there. The words she flung at him were like stones, and he flinched with each bruising blow.

Karl stalked towards Malina. His fist slammed into her stomach and she bent forward with a pained cry before looking up at him with her bloody teeth bared.

"Give us a kiss then," she said, pouting her lips at him.

He swung the axe. Her body crumpled as her head separated from her shoulders. The swing's strength had it roll away and land at Father Bauer's feet. It looked up at him and the mouth twitched in one final, feral grin before the eyes became unfocused and the mouth still.

The two men stared at the body as blood first gushed, and then seeped, from the mangled neck. Father Bauer avoided looking at the head at his feet, bile rising to sting his throat.

"Go, Father. I will deal with the mess," Karl said. His stern voice vibrated with a gruff energy.

"I didn't get to give her absolution," he whispered.

Karl's eyes were dark. "She was beyond it," he said. "Now go."

Father Bauer was not in the habit of taking orders from his flock, but he did as he was told. He stood up, legs shaking as if he were a newborn foal, and climbed the rickety stairs. As he ascended back up into the civilized light, he saw from the corner of his eye Karl sink to his knees beside Malina's corpse. His large hands grasped her roughly by her small and slender shoulders and he lifted her up almost effortlessly. The priest wondered if it was just a trick of the light, strange shadows caused by the weak candlelight, that made him see Karl throw back his head and hungrily bite with forceful teeth into the trickling flesh of Malina's neck.

He closed the door at the top of the stairs. The five men stared at him, eyes wide. Nervous sweat rolled down Father Bauer's face, and he mopped at it with his sleeve.

"Do not go down there," he said to them. They glanced at each other in consternation.

"Is it...?"

"She is dead," Father Bauer gasped out. "Karl is dealing with her remains. Do not disturb him." He fled the house then, leaving the men standing there.

The early winter sun had begun to set, its pale light ceding ground to the dark. A watery full moon rose above the treeline, casting long shadows of the jagged pines onto the dirt of the road. They reminded him of long, sharp teeth snapping at his heels and chasing him home. Something in the depths of him howled at it, filling him up with a primeval song that reverberated down his limbs and into his fingertips. He quickened his steps, eager to get back to the safety of the house of God.

His mind stumbled over the terrible events of the day, Malina's words echoing in his mind again and again, replaying Karl's mouth sinking into her slim neck. He was so consumed by the thoughts and feelings that boiled within him that he did not notice his feet had changed direction and he was heading back in the opposite direction from the church. He didn't come to his senses until he found himself knocking at a familiar door. The widow Koch opened it.

Her wide, surprised eyes looked up at him from beneath long, light lashes. "Father? What are you doing here?"

"You were there today," he said, and his stomach tightened as lust pooled there. "You saw everything."

Her eyebrows raised, and her lips puckered in a surprised smile. "I was," she said.

"Are you well? How are you feeling?" he said worriedly.

"I'm fine, Father, just fine," she said reassuringly, and then she reached out to take his weathered hand in hers. Her eyes smoldered as she stared into his, and she lifted his hand to her lips. Instead of kissing it, like she had so often before, she brought his index finger to her lips. She drew it into her mouth, sucking gently at first and then harder, her clever tongue swirling around it. He found himself growing harder and harder until it was practically painful. He pictured himself pushing her inside, locking the door behind them, ripping her clothes off until he buried himself in her with unrestrained ecstasy.

He stared at her, and she pulled back, nipping at his fingertip as she did so. She panted, her chest heaving, her eyes burning with something he had only ever heard about in hushed tones in the halls of the seminary school he had attended so very long ago.

"Won't you come in?" she asked in a husky voice.

And he did.

SMALL POTATOES

THE SUN HAS set by the time I escape from my evening exam, and I grab a late dinner as the remains of my English lit course leak out my ears. Once I'm nestled back in the lumpy twin bed of my student dorm, my takeout ramen steaming on my small and messy desk, I finally call my parents. My father picks up the video call, giving me a picturesque view of their Idaho farm in the background. I hear machinery in the background, raised voices calling out to one another in a friendly manner. It must be planting day, their work extending into dusk, and I politely ask what's going into the ground this year.

"A new variety of test potato," he says, holding up a seed potato, the miniature version of a potato they will plant in the fields. "A small russet. Government contract, genetically engineered. Very cool." The potato gleams ruby red in the light as the sun sets over the mountains in the distance. He turns it this way and that so I can get a better view. "Isn't it beautiful?"

I have not inherited my parent's love for produce, or for the back-breaking labour that goes into the growing of it. I dream of being a journalist, a philosopher, an artist—something more thoughtful and less pedestrian than a potato farmer.

"It's supposed to multiply faster and grow twice as many potatoes. It's like a strawberry plant—it sends out runners to form new mother plants..."

I interrupt him then, and ask to talk to Mom. Her sweaty forehead, plastered with runaway strands of grey hair, pops into view.

"Hi sweetie! We love you!" Her voice makes me ache with homesickness, and we talk to each other for a few minutes about how my exam went and my plans for the weekend.

"Will you be coming home anytime soon?" they chorus. There's so much hope on their faces, and I can barely stand to burst it like a bubble in the palm of my hand. "Sorry, guys, it's an accelerated program, remember? I start summer courses almost immediately." They visibly deflate.

"Small potatoes," My mother says, though I can see in their eyes it's a bigger deal than they're making of it. It's always been one of their favourite sayings, an old joke they haven't realized has outstayed its welcome with me. I resist the urge to roll my eyes.

We chat for another half hour as I slurp my noodles. After a while, they tell me they have to run—it's planting season, of course, and if they want to keep this government contract, they need to keep on schedule. I promise we'll talk soon. We hang up, and my dorm room seems small and claustrophobic then, guilt settling like dust on my belongings about my reluctance to return home. I ignore it, instead queuing up a video on my phone.

I stay on for the summer term, and besides a few emails back and forth and the daily texts from both of my parents, I don't video chat with them for several weeks. It's hard during the early season—potatoes require a surprising amount of work, and when you're doing test fields, everything has to be documented. It's a tremendous amount of paperwork and eats up their time. When I finally decide on a bored afternoon to give them a call, they don't pick up. I frown and send a quick text message asking them to call me back.

It takes them over an hour to return my call. By then, I'm anxious, and I snap at them when I pick up. As their only child, I'm used to being their centre of attention, no matter what season it is. "Where were you?"

"Sorry, we were out in the fields," Mom says. They look guilty. More than that, they look tired. My mother's forehead has more lines than I remember, and her eyes are tired. My father's bald head is red and peeling. Giant flakes of skin litter the shoulders of his dark, stained shirt. His beard is scraggly and unkempt. They look like they've been run ragged.

They start talking about hilling, how the new potatoes are proving to be a challenge and they are having to adjust a lot of their long-standing farming practices for this new variety. I interrupt them.

"You guys look exhausted. Is everything okay?"

They glance at each other, and I see in their eyes a conversation they are having silently, one of the benefits of having been married to each other for twenty years. Their telepathic connection has always annoyed me; I don't like to feel left out.

"It's nothing," my mother says. "Just farm stuff. I know you don't like hearing about it."

"Small potatoes," Dad agrees.

"I'm just worried about you guys," I say.

My father breaks into a grin then, his white teeth shining through the thick dark wire of his beard. "It's a parent's job to worry about their children, not the other way around." Mom nods along. "We're just getting old and set in our ways. There's nothing to get all worked up about."

"Small potatoes," Mom echoes again.

I look between the two of them and let it lie.

"How are things with you?" Dad asks, and we fall into a comfortable routine, the anxiety souring my stomach beginning to settle.

Their texts become even less frequent. I don't realize at first. I'm too busy socializing and studying. It isn't until I realize I haven't heard from them at all in several days that I start to really worry.

When I call, they are sitting together on the couch. Dad holds the phone at a weird angle.

"Hey guys, is everything okay?" I don't even begin with niceties. "I haven't heard from you in days. Is something wrong?"

Mom's eyes are strange.

"Small potatoes," my father says, his face slack.

"Stop saying that, something is very clearly wrong." My voice cracks in my panic.

My mother looks off screen, her lips moving silently.

"Will you come home?" Dad asks.

"I'll come home as soon as I can," I tell him. "Please, just tell me what's wrong."

"Goodbye," he says.

The call ends. They don't pick up when I call back.

I'm already making arrangements to rush home when I get an email. My professor is having a family emergency, and class is suspended for two weeks while they scramble to find a replacement. I have my plane tickets booked within minutes.

I text my childhood best friend from the airport, asking him to drive by the house. He does and tells me the fields are in good form, and my parents' trucks are there, and a harvester is in the field, but it hasn't moved since he saw it last week. Nobody answered when he knocked at the front door, but he had to get to work and couldn't linger. I wait at my gate, my legs bouncing nervously, staring at the screen, wishing more than ever that I had gone home when they first asked.

The plane arrives, and I board. As soon as we're clear, I check my phone every thirty seconds. The thread of our conversation is just dozens of my messages lying unread and unanswered. I call the police, but they brush me off. If something had happened or something was truly wrong, my parents' workers would have notified them, and they haven't heard anything.

I catch an Uber after we land. It deposits me at the mailbox at the end of the driveway—the guy doesn't want to drive the long and winding gravel road up to the house. He says something about his tires, but I'm too anxious to get out to pay attention to him. I slam the car door behind me. I don't even wait until he's driven off before I throw my backpack onto my shoulders and start making the long walk up to the old farmhouse with its peeling white paint over yellow bricks and green trim.

I climb the creaking stairs to the front door. The sun is setting, and the old porch light flickers on. A moth begins beating against it almost immediately, its white wings fluttering in desperation. I can't help but wonder if it's an omen. The screen door still hangs at an odd angle—Dad has been saying he'll replace the loose door hinges for over a year now. I hesitate before the oak, wondering if I should knock, my fist hovering about the surface of the door. I have never knocked on my own front door, and I don't know why I'm about to start. I swallow down the strange feeling and decide to just go in.

It's unlocked, which is not unusual. We never lock the door. It's what I open the door to that is unusual. The front hall is littered with leaves and dust. A few thick footprints—my father's farm boots, I think—are in them, but even those are also covered with another, thinner layer of dust.

Mom would *never* let her house get in this kind of state.

Half of my childhood memories are of her with a dust cloth or a mop in hand. I can hear her voice in my head; "Just because we live on a farm, doesn't mean we have to live like pigs."

My voice cracks as I call out. "Mom? Dad? Are you there? I'm home."

There is no answer. The light outside is fading fast, and I can see a dim light from the living room. I enter the house and take a few hesitant steps towards it. The lamp is on—my grandmother's lamp, all dripping beads with a velvet lampshade, a tacky old thing I've always hated. My eyes catch on its gaudiness before I finally see them.

My parents are sitting on the couch together, their shoulders touching. Mom's wearing her overalls over an old fun-run shirt. Her hair is in two long, badly done and loose grey braids under a ripped bandana. Dad is in torn and dirty pants, his worn work boots still on.

"Mom? Dad? It's me. I'm home." I take a step towards them.

In unison, they turn towards me. They look wrong, *are* wrong.

"I thought I'd come home to surprise you," I continue. My mouth is dry. "It sounded like you needed me."

My mother opens her mouth as if to reply, but nothing comes out. Her movements are jerky, stuttering. Her mouth gapes, wide and dark and empty. Her tongue whips from side to side.

"Mom? Are you okay?" I feel like throwing up, and I move towards her. A wave of stench rolls over me, and I pause. My hand goes to my pocket, searching for my phone, ready to call 911. With horror, I realize I left it in the back seat of the Uber.

"Will you come home?" Dad says to me from his spot on the couch next to her. His eyes are like craters in his face. His mouth moves, the words too wide, the voice cracked and raw. "Will you come home?"

"Dad, I *am* home." My heart pounds, the words like weights on my lips. "What's going on?"

I can see from where I'm standing that they are covered in large, fleshy bumps. That horrible smell, which I quickly recognize as the smell of rotting potatoes, emanates from where they sit on the couch. When I take another step forward, their heads lurch towards me in tandem, but they do not stand up. The outlines of their bodies have softened, the skin hanging in folds as if empty. I throw up into my mouth as liquid seeps down from their limbs, and as I move closer, I realize that what I'm seeing are not my parents, not anymore. They are marionettes, empty shells puppeteer'd by whatever horror grew in the deep, damp soil of their beloved farm. They are oozing around the edges, as if the back of them has liquefied, staining the couch. The smell of it is awful, horrible, like the leftover potatoes left at the bottom of a forgotten bag at the back of the pantry. From the back of their necks hangs a thin white strand of vegetable matter. It is long and limp, coiled around itself as it stretches through the house and out the open back door to the potato fields.

I start to scream then, and that's when the large bumps growing out of my parents' skin open, and dozens of eyes blink at me blearily. They are my parents' eyes, replicated over and over and over again, and they all turn to look at me. Without warning, three of the eyes burst like overripe fruit, viscous fluid spitting out, and things like snakes, long and vine-like runners, unroll from where they've erupted, reaching towards me.

I don't stop screaming and scramble backwards. My many-eyed parents don't move from their place on the couch. One of my mother's tendrils wraps around my ankle. It is cold and dry and small hairs probe at my skin. I yank my foot out of it, and it breaks, oozing brown liquid.

All of my parents' eyes blink in unison at me as I stop just out of reach. My father's mouth opens again.

"Will you come home? Will you come home?" His words are staccato shotgun blasts to my heart. More of his eyes burst, sending forth tendrils that reach for me. I'm sobbing now, snot and tears mixing as I turn around and flee the house, pushing through the screen door and knocking it fully off its hinges. It clatters to the deck, and I reach across it to pull the thick oak door shut.

I run back to the driveway, brain stuttering. I stand there, chest heaving, and take a moment to throw up the shitty airplane food. The acrid smell of it and the bile now spattering my white sneakers brings me out of my panic for a moment. I look back at the house. My parents' silhouettes are still visible from their place where they have become fused to the couch. A long tendril reaches up to tap against the windowpane, calling me in.

Grief hits me then—grief and rage, and a cold calm settles over me as I decide what to do. I run to the garage, where I know my father keeps a dozen fully stocked gas cans of both regular and diesel fuel. I grab one in each hand along with a pack of matches and run back to the house, the cans sloshing.

I start pouring them around the exterior, splashing it over the deck railing. I pour it onto my mother's prize hydrangeas, and shove down the memory of her fertilizing them, a tender look on her face.

I hesitate at the front door before opening it. There are several runners still searching blindly in the hallway for me. I toss the gasoline on them, too. The keys to all the different tractors hang from the hooked shelf in the shape of a sheep that my father built for my mother when they were still newly engaged. I grab a bunch of them and then take a step back.

With trembling fingers, I take the matches out of my shorts pocket. The first one doesn't light, and I drop it. The smell of gasoline burns my nostrils.

"Will you come home?" my father calls from the next room.

I fumble and break the second match, but the third match catches. I debate whether I want to peek my head into the living room and see them one last time. Mom makes a gagging noise, and I think of all of those eyes turning to look at me as she burns, and I decide against it. I drop the match and turn around to walk out the door. The fire catches with a soft *whoompf*, and I make sure to leave the door open for better airflow. I don't stay to watch my parents ignite.

I walk to the barn, my strides long and purposeful. It's a newer building, all sleek metal and smoothly opening doors. I spent my teenage years farming, and walking into the barn is like a different sort of homecoming. The massive tractor is front and centre, with the oversized tiller already attached and waiting. It dawns on me then that my parents knew what was happening, knew what was coming. No farmer would till his crop under unless he absolutely had to. They just never got the chance. I am numb as I climb inside the tractor and start it with a practiced turn of the key. My foot on the gas pedal, I exit the barn directly into the field.

I'm glad I am seated far above it. Below me, the ground is covered in potato bushes, with strawberry-like runners creating an aboveground network of crisscrossed wires, lines of communication and contamination that are visibly pulsing. The tiller and I set to work.

The sun has fully set now, and the tractor headlights illuminate the carnage in front of me while the house burns behind me. The runners wiggle like exposed earthworms in the beams of light before they go beneath the wheels and the tillers and are chopped into small pieces.

I can't tell if it's the whir of the machinery cutting into the flesh of the potatoes, or if they are screaming. The high-pitched whining noise reaches a fever pitch, and the outside of the tractor is splattered with thick, viscous green fluid that smells like chlorophyll. I stare ahead, driving in tight turns. I do the ten acres of test field in what feels like forever and yet no time at all before I pull up to the driveway again and drive onto it. I don't want to step onto the soil. Behind me, the field is weeping, a gruesome mix of chopped potato bushes, lumps of red-skinned potatoes and soil. All of it is oozing a green blood-like fluid. The whining noise has stopped in the wake of the carnage I have wrought, and I'm grateful for it.

When stepping down to the gravel, I nearly land on a body lying in the fetal position. He is just off to the side, next to a decorative rhododendron. A long tendril protruding from his lower spine leads towards the field, where it ends in a ragged cut.

I don't recognize him, and I'm glad for it. He lies there on the grass, his runner bleeding that strange green fluid mixed with red blood, both of them swirled together like an ice cream cone from the local Dairy Queen. He is small and withered, his skin a sickly green from what I assume is a buildup of solanine. Despite his near-mummification, a few dry eyes still watch my every move, though the ones in his face remain closed and sunken. He breathes raspily. I stare at him mutely before crossing the drive to where I had tossed a red jug. There's still some liquid in it, which I pour onto his body and light another match.

He doesn't scream, doesn't whine. He just burns. He smells almost like a baked potato. As he dies, I wonder how many of the farmhands were in the field when I tilled it, lying above or below the soil. I wonder if they felt pain as I minced them, or if they were beyond that. I am so very tired, and I sink to the ground next to the burning man, and start to sob again.

When the first of the emergency vehicles arrives, I am out of tears, my eyes blankly reflecting nothing but the flames engulfing my childhood home. The reek of blood and plant matter is still rising from the fields. Behind the police cars and firetrucks is a fleet of white vans and people in hazmat suits. A further train of black vehicles arrives, spitting out grim-faced men in tailored black suits. They lead me away from the ashes of my life, and I let them. I look back over my shoulder only once. I see that the people in hazmat suits are pouring liquid from large jugs over the field, throwing the empty ones in the back of a tractor trailer as they remove pallets of them from another.

I'm checked over at a hospital. People talk around me. I stare at the wall. The men in black suits visit me, talking sternly. I don't even hear them, just numbly nod and sign the papers they shove at me. They take me back to the airport and put me on a plane. I don't speak a word to anyone for several weeks. There is no funeral.

I take a leave of absence from school. No one even knows that I went back home, or that I was there. They know only that there was a terrible fire and my parents and their farmhands didn't survive. People look at me with pity now. My bank account suddenly reads seven figures, and I know it for what it is: hush money.

Eventually, I start to play pretend. I go back to class and look at job listings that I don't apply to. I open my mouth to put food in it, start brushing my hair and bathing again. I even start talking to my friends again. But I'm not normal, and after many months, when the snow begins to melt into small rivers that crisscross the concourse, my friends start to notice when I withdraw again. They stage meetings, hangouts so that we can talk, but I don't want to talk. I can't.

My friend Anastasia looks at me from across the coffee shop table. "I know you've been through a lot," she says softly. She reaches out a manicured hand to hold mine. I yank it away. "But you've become so distant again. I'm here, if you want to talk. Is there something wrong?"

I stare at her mutely. I can't tell her that something is inside me. I can feel it there, writing beneath the skin, something that has been slowly growing over the course of the winter, a long, thin tendril crawling up my nerve pathways from my ankle to take root in my brain. More and more, I find that my actions, and now even my words, are not always my own. My tongue moves, but my brain is screaming, fighting against the syllables that my mouth forms against my will.

"It's just small potatoes," I say to her. "I wouldn't worry about it."

PROMETHEUS'S JARS

ON CHRISTMAS DAY the year I turned nine, my father gave me a gift from his laboratory. He did not know it was Christmas—I doubt he knew what year it was, or how old I was. I rarely saw him. He lived in the darkest corner of the house, in a secluded room lit only by a single lamp. This was his lair, the cave in which he remained and from which all of my memories of him derive.

I hated that room. When he emerged from behind the steel door that separated him from the world, he would blink, and a mottled hand, stained by preservatives and other chemicals, would rise to cover his eyes. His goggled face was alien to me. Skeletally thin, his body constantly trembled, his movements jerky and uncoordinated. We were not close; I barely knew him. He made no attempt to get to know me. Our relationship was defined, I think, by our fear of one other. He was consumed by whatever strange works took place in that dreaded room.

Once, when I was younger still, he'd brought me into it, this biologist's lair. The strong smell of preserving chemicals and ammonia had blurred my vision, and when my watering eyes finally cleared, I was greeted by the stuff of nightmares: shelves lined all four walls of the room, filled with

assorted specimens, floating in jars. Snakes, pigeons, rats, eels, salamanders, and frogs gazed down at me like regimented soldiers.

They seemed to breathe, their tiny chests rising with each watery breath. And they did not seem dead, only sleeping, floating in liquid dreams. I'd half-expected them to turn to me in greeting, with phosphorescent eyes that burned in the dark. But they didn't, and quickly I had fled my father and his room, the steel door shutting like a trap behind me.

"I have almost done it," he said to me that Christmas morning, his tremulous voice cracking with strain. I had knocked on his door to wish him a Happy Christmas, and he'd thrown it open, his spectral body emerging out of the dark like some evil apparition. "I have almost done it." In his arms, he clutched one of his specimen jars. "Here, have him. Have him, son." He thrust it into my sticky hands. *"Alligator mississippienis. Juvenile. Good Specimen. Near perfect,"* he breathed reverently.

I stood there awkwardly, the baby alligator in its jar curled in my arms like a child.

"Almost there," my father said again, eyes wild. "So close."

And with those final words, he retreated back into his cave and refused to come out for the rest of the day. Mother and I enjoyed our Christmas dinner alone, my father's place at the table abandoned and empty as usual.

That night, I placed the baby alligator, whom I had christened "Alvie", on my bedside table, much to my mother's discontent. She kissed my forehead and tucked me in before softly closing my bedroom door, leaving Alvi and me alone. The pale moonlight that usually filtered in through the window was hidden, and my nightlight cast an eerie, pallid glow. Branches scratched against my windowpane and dark, pregnant clouds flitted across the sky like the shadows of an owl. I wasn't scared, however, and soon my eyes grew heavy and closed.

Just as I began to drift off, a curious sound began.

Thud.

Thud.

Thud.

I raised my head briefly off of my pillow and looked at my closet. The noise ceased. I was not a superstitious child, afraid of monsters or ghosts. My eyes closed again, and I began to dream.

Thud.

Thud.

Thud.

The noise was coming from my bedside table.

I sleepily turned to look at Alvie. His eyes, previously closed, had opened. Yellow reptilian eyes peered into mine. Terror gripped me. Those eyes, lit with a primeval savagery, held me captive. His tiny jaw opened, revealing a grin studded with tiny, sharp teeth. A bleached tongue pressed through them, and his scaly paw rose towards me. His muscular tail had uncurled from between his legs, and he was rhythmically pounding it against the bottom of his jar.

Thud.

Thud.

Thud.

I screamed.

"Your father is very sick," Mother said as she packed my things, "and the sickness is in his brain. You've seen the way Papa shakes. It is making him see things that aren't there. It happens only in a few people, but your father has it very bad."

I knew on some level that the incident with the baby alligator had something to do with it. My "overactive imagination" had been "triggered by the gifts of a madman". I left Alvie sitting on my bedside table.

Father died a year later. Mother went back to the house just once, in order to retrieve some trinket of her mother's she had forgotten. Instead of her trinket, she found my father's desiccated corpse, several weeks expired, lying in the hallway to the kitchen. In his obsession, he had stopped feeding himself and died of starvation. The event—despite the hardship she had endured and the resentment she carried toward him—was highly traumatic for her. For weeks afterwards, she was quiet and withdrawn.

It was a closed-casket funeral.

Life went on. I grew up and excelled in school. I was accepted to one of the top universities in the country, where I was an honours student double-majoring in biology and chemistry and was well-liked and popular among my classmates and professors. Life was perfect, though in the dim recesses of my psyche, Alvie and that ominous steel door lurked. I had recurring nightmares that would send me reeling upright in the middle of the night, drenched in sweat and screaming while ghostly alligators and vast, grinning jaws swam in my vision.

I was twenty-one years old, recently graduated with honours and accepted to a graduate school on the West Coast when the symptoms began. Trembling, sweating, fumbling. Sometimes I would shake so hard the headboard of my bed would slam against the wall. Walking became painful, and my muscles cramped and seized. I began to stutter. The symptoms were severe with sudden onset. My mother took me to doctors. "We don't know, we don't know", they said as they ran their tests and prodded me with needle fingers. Finally, I was given a diagnosis.

"Early on-set Parkinson's," one doctor said. My mother clapped a hand to her mouth and began to weep. "Rather severe," he continued. "Of course, there is some evidence of a genetic tendency..."

The ghost of my father rose into my mind unbidden, and his spindly, shaking fingers reached out to draw me close. The doctor's voice broke through this devilled hallucination: "it's rapid advance...leads me to believe...followed by hallucination, dementia, slurring of the speech...no more than a year and a half...expectancy."

Without a word, I rose and strode out of the doctor's office. With Mother's cries echoing behind me, I fled into the night.

I wandered in a daze, neither thinking nor feeling. A strange disengagement from myself came over me as my diagnosis sank in. I paused only once, to stare at my reflection in a storefront window. In it, I saw my father, and I could not help but cry.

I do not know what brought me there, but I eventually found myself in front of my childhood home. What had once been a beautiful suburb was now a row of dilapidated, boarded-up houses the city couldn't be bothered to bulldoze quite yet. Perhaps I sought that comfort, that invincibility every child feels at the beginning of their lives, or perhaps it was my father's ghost—and the horrible legacy he had left—drawing me back.

The paint had peeled and stained a dingy grey. Shutters hung askew, and the cracked and grimy windows allowed no glimpses into the inside. The porch sagged, the grass dead and limp. The vibrant life maintained by my mother's gentle touch was long gone; only fitting decay remained. I took a deep breath and entered through the unlocked door.

The house appeared different but yet surprisingly undisturbed—no graffiti painted the walls, no evidence of teenage trespassers littered the floor. The rotting floorboards creaked underfoot as I padded from room to room, guided by memory. Mold was king here; despite its fecundity, it remained a grim reminder for me of my own impending death.

The only thing that remained unchanged was that single, intimidating steel door leading into the depths of my father's own madness.

I would not go there.

In one of the kitchen drawers, I found an ancient flashlight, and my shaking hands somehow managed to turn it on. I climbed the stairs to my old room, hoping to find some comfort in my childhood retreat.

The rusty knob to my room broke off in my hands. I leaned my shoulder into the door. It gave with a good shove. I found I could not straighten up after—the disease had begun to seize my muscles and cause hunching. I felt...hollow.

My room was unchanged, except for a very heavy layer of dust that coated everything. It seemed no one had entered this room since my departure twelve years ago. A single bubblegum wrapper lay on the ground from where I'd thrown it while watching my mother pack my things.

And there, on my bedside dresser, was Alvie's glass jar, so thick with dust that the contents were invisible. My father's final gift.

I crossed to the jar and stood before it. The nightmare from many years ago surfaced, but I hesitated only briefly before I reached out a hand and wiped the dust off of it.

In it, Alvie lay as I remembered him, curled up in a pale imitation of sleep. His prehistoric tail lay curved between his tiny legs. How strange he looked, floating there as if he were in his native element. I sighed in relief, touching the jar again with my forefinger.

Alvie opened his eyes.

Fear froze me in a tight embrace. His eyes opened wider, and he *smiled* at me. Needle-sharp teeth gleamed. I trembled even harder. His toothy grin grew wider and his powerful tail rapped against the bottom of his jar in greeting.

Thud.

Thud.

Thud.

With a cry, I fled the room and downstairs, where I stood shaking in the mildewed kitchen, the old flashlight clutched in my hands. From upstairs, the cry of a baby alligator echoed through the house. I shut my eyes tight, and everything fell silent again.

Then, the rustling began. The sound of skin brushing against skin and against glass filled the air. It was a quiet sound, and underneath it all was the sound of water, like gentle waves against a shore. I hesitated, but the noise did not stop, and I resolved then to find whatever was causing it. Gathering up my courage, I wrapped my arms around my chest and padded down the hall, ears cocked, heart pounding. The sounds led me to the familiar steel door. The rustling came from behind it.

I dreaded going any further. All these years later, were his specimens still there? What waited for me behind it? I swallowed my fear and opened the door.

In the dark, the dreamers stirred. As my flashlight moved around the room, it revealed the pickled creatures suspended in their jars on shelf after shelf; they moved in reaction to the light, pushing up against the walls of their glass prisons. The sound of lapping liquid intensified, and the combined noises rose to a crescendo that echoed in my ears. Pale ghosts, bleached white, stared down at me with interested eyes.

From upstairs, the cry of the baby alligator came again. I shivered, standing there in my father's laboratory, and wept as these creatures turned their gazes upon me. The flashlight continued to swing around the room until it found the one place where no pale abomination lay—my father's desk. On it, coated in the same thick dust that coated everything else in the house, was a leather-bound book. I crossed to it, rubbery legs making the going slow and difficult. A hundred eyes watched my progress.

I blew the dust from the book's cover and flipped open the journal to find my father's cramped, spidery handwriting filling every page. Calculations, sketches, names of chemical compounds... Father's scientific testament to a battle against death. Many things were crossed out, and towards the end, a singles list was circled multiple times. "*So close*", the writing next to it said, a familiar mantra. "*I have almost conquered the madness that is decay. I have managed to reverse the spinal and neural degeneration, even enriching it in some specimens. They show intelligence uncommon to their species. I have halted death and brought a half-life to these poor creatures, these tiny miracles which I cherish more than my own flesh and blood. This disease that is hidden within my blood—soon, it will be conquered. I will live again. Just a few more ingredients...and it will be perfect.*"

I gripped the edges of the desk, almost dizzy. Father had attempted to stop death in its tracks, and what's more, he had almost *succeeded*. The creatures around me, these victories over nature, they were his legacy. A legacy he had left to me. Was it in fact madness, or the madness of genius that eventually drove my mother away? He had nearly conquered the demon of his flesh, the demon that had passed to me. Was he so close to a cure?

My blood ran hot and my veins writhed like snakes beneath my skin.

The alligator cried again, but I wasn't afraid anymore.

My father's final list of ingredients was on the last page. Beside each item was an explanation on what it did and how it reacted with the other chemicals coupled with a minor electrical current. My mind ran through them, and understanding fell into place. With each cramped sentence, I understood how he did it...how *I* could do it. I could reverse the damage done to my brain. I could give myself a second chance at life, like he attempted to give himself.

Father was so close, but his science was so antiquated. Missing those final ingredients, he could not instill proper, everlasting life into these poor creatures in their jars. But I...I, with my schooling in modern-day chemistry and biology, with knowledge that had been unavailable to him, I could do this.

In my father's darkened laboratory, I began to laugh.

I have cut off contact with my mother. She wept when I told her of Father's experiment and what he had accomplished, and of what I intended to complete. She was not joyous like I expected her to be: was her husband not an unrecognized genius? Was her son not given a second chance to keep his hold on a tenuous life? Did these things not matter?

Evidently not: she sobbed and believed that I, like my father, had gone mad. It was not a discovery. Rather, it was a symptom, and she begged me to come back to her for treatment. I swore at her and hung up the phone. I have avoided all contact with her since.

I live within my father's house now. Alvie sits on the desk, a position of honour reserved for Father's prime specimen, and the greatest gift he ever gave me. I am so close. I am almost ready. My body is weaker than ever, and my eyes burn bright with a fire that rages beneath my skin. I am constantly trembling, evidence of the degenerative disease that eats away at my mind. The loss of motor function has hindered me, but my father's specimens comfort me with wordless whispers.

I will not die. I will continue my father's work. My life will be restored. Shivering, I will take off my robe and stand naked before the great tank I have procured and filled with Father's potions. I will descend into it slowly, stiffly, and the preservatives will seep beneath my skin, burn the life back into me. I will remain immortal in my own tub of dreams until such a time as I can emerge, metamorphosed, surrounded by my father's miracles. I have perfected his recipe, and I will not die.

Around me, my brothers stir in their slumber. Alvie slowly winks at me and raps his tail three times against his watery prison in silent approval.

Thud.

Thud.

Thud.

I can hear his heart beating.

Nyctophobia

It is a well-accepted fact that most children go through a period in their lives where they're afraid of the dark. Closets, basements, and the dusty space under the bed all become the territories of nightmares. It is an evolutionary warning tattooed into the mind of all humans when they are very young: not everyone who goes into the dark comes back out again.

The house had a reputation. Josiah knew this. It had mouldered for twenty years after the trial and would have mouldered for twenty more if not for the historical society and an investor who thought the scene of the crimes would be an excellent, if tasteless, setting for a museum about the history of human violence. For the past year, tradesmen had poured in and out of it, shoring up beams, tidying up the facade, fixing the interior. Now they needed a hot-water heater repair, and Josiah was the one on call.

He grabbed his tools from the back of the van and made his way to the front porch. No one was on site today, so he quickly plugged in the code of the lockbox, drew out the heavy tarnished key, and opened the worn wooden door. The inside was surprisingly bright—sun shone through large windows that still had the manufacturer's stickers attached. Despite the cleanliness, the boxes of unassembled furniture, and the workmen's

tools left over the weekend, the place was strangely eerie and filled him with dread. Unsettled, he ventured deeper into the house.

He found the door marked "Basement—Staff Only" and opened it to a wall of solid black. It was like staring into a void, and he could not repress a shiver. He realized he was blocking the light and stepped off to the side, peering around the frame as his eyes adjusted. No light-switch, but if he squinted, he could see the faded outline of a hanging bulb and a dangling string, reminiscent of a hangman's noose. God, he wished he hadn't forgotten his flashlight. Straightening his back, he steeled himself, muttering to himself that he was not a silly, superstitious child who was afraid of the dark. Not anymore, at least.

The stairs groaned underfoot. They were intact, thank goodness, but he was a bulky man and did not want to test their resilience—or his luck—too thoroughly. He stepped nimbly down them, ignoring the sudden swirl of anxiety in his stomach. He stepped off the last stair and onto the floor.

And suddenly, he understood what it was like to be prey.

The hairs along his entire body rose. Primeval fear gripped him as something *wrong* stared at him from the shadows, stared *into* him, and found him worthy of consumption. Bile rose from his stomach. The surrounding blackness swirled. Josiah nearly choked on the darkness threatening to pour down his throat like ink. It was evil—pure and simple, the absence of good and of light and of life.

The lightbulb hung four feet in front of him and he dove for it. His fingers grasped at it as the void closed in. After an eternity, his fingers caught on the errant string and he yanked. The bulb flickered to life, and Josiah envisioned its small yellow moon banishing the entity back into the shadows. His mind's eye created a shifting nightmare—it was a man, it was a monster, it was a deep-sea denizen with long fangs that were dry and thirsting, and then a man again, leering, with too many teeth pressing out against bloated black lips.

He stood there trembling, his breath hitching, tears threatening to spill onto the chalky ground. His heart thudded in his chest, and his eyes strained to look into the dark (*why was it still so dark?*) outside of the lightbulb's influence. Boxes and strange shapes draped in rotted sheets lined the walls. His gaze snagged at the top of the stairs, the rectangle beacon of the door washing the top few steps in pale light. A way out of the dark—an ascent back into God's grace.

His joints locked, the oppressive atmosphere and his terror holding him in place better than any shackles could. His eyes stayed trained on the door. Something in the corners shifted ever so slightly, and he was released. Josiah bolted from the safety of the light and made for the stairs. It was a short leap to the bottom, the step threatening to buckle beneath him. He fell forward, his hands scrabbling as fast as his feet, a desperate crawl that drove large splinters into his palms. He could feel the sting of cuts, the welling of blood, and his brain shrieked a wordless warning. Whatever-it-was could smell the salt and copper, would know that he was wounded and afraid and *oh so very alone.*

He reached the top and pulled himself upright, relief and adrenaline flooding his veins. Now in the arms of safety, he gave a giddy chuckle before facing the basement, leaning against the newly installed doorframe. Only a few minutes must have passed since he'd first descended—the lightbulb was still gently swaying. Silhouetted in the light, Josiah understood that no fresh drywall or new flooring could cover the sin in this house. Nothing could erase the history that had seeped into its walls or wash away the blood in its floors. It was a house of ghosts, and would remain so.

"The devil lives down there," he whispered to himself as he stared back into hell, trembling, trying to compose himself, his limbs turned to liquid and his joints to jelly. "The devil lives down there," he said again, voice steadying, before what vaguely resembled a hand grabbed his ankle and dragged him screaming back into the devouring dark.

MYCELIUM GHOST

WHEN SHE DIED, he buried her in the soft loam beneath a stand of pine trees, chopping at their roots with the blade of his shovel until they ceded enough ground that he could drop her in. She lay curled in the fetal position in the sacred womb of the earth, her eyes open but empty. She was still inside of herself when he threw the first shovelful of dirt back over her.

Within days, nature reclaimed her, her mouth opening post-mortem as a colony of mushrooms took up residence at the base of her skull and the forest began to colonize her. Who she had once been leaked out into the dense network of roots and mycelium surrounding her body and tapping into it. Her consciousness became one with the woodland. Whispers of trees ran through her veins as they fed on her, turning her sugars into fertilizer.

She quickly forgot what it was like to be human—to be alone, without the chatter of ferns, or the deep, slow not-words of the trees, confined to a single body and a single mind. She wandered extensively through the expansive universe of the forest floor. She became a thought, a whisper herself that flitted through the being of each living thing connected to the intricate threads that bound them all together.

She visited the spongy mushroom caps that stuck their heads out from the dense carpet of decaying pine needles. She pulsed up pine trees, sliding through their sap and resting in their boughs. She explored the vegetation, the small brush and bushes that tenderly reached out their new roots to tap into the spores that spread their way through the dark and fertile ground. The forest welcomed her.

There was nothing but existence, and every moment was forever, and forever just a moment. She had sunk completely into the ecosystem. She flew through the branches, leaping from tree to tree using a million miles of secret highways and roads, the long strands of mycorrhizal fungi that lay underneath the lovely rich soil. Where she existed, she didn't feel the press of time. She had no idea how long she had been not-alive but more limitlessly alive than she had ever been when *he* returned to the woods.

The trees told her first. Trees have a long memory, and so they had not forgotten the stranger who had brought her to them. The leaves rustled, told her to go home to where her husk lay, and to wait there until she remembered. It would be worth it, they said. She listened.

She hadn't been in her body for so long—it was a little out of the way, and when she spread back into it, sinking into the desiccated strands of muscle, the still-solid bones, it was like putting on an old sweater that one had outgrown; comforting in its familiarity, but slightly shrunken and limiting. Her body was her origin point, so she could still feel the strands reassuringly connecting her to the forest.

Abigail. She had been Abigail. She had come to the woods for...a convergence. A meeting. A date.

The mycelium that had grown down her throat fluttered in excitement. She, Abbey, had come here for a date.

Good, the trees told her in their wordless way. *Keep going.*

She remembered walking down a long winding trail through the cathedral of trees. The sunlight had filtered down through the branches, speckling the path ahead of her with gold. She'd tried to focus on the beauty of the moment, because her feet hurt. She had worn cute flats. It was a fourth date, and he wanted to surprise her with a visit to his favourite place. She had expected a restaurant or cafe. She hadn't expected a hike. Her heels had ached, blisters quickly forming, but she didn't want to take off her shoes and get her feet dirty. Her current state of being scoffed at that—how could she not want to be skin to skin with the world and intimate with the woods?

She remembered a man on the path ahead of her. Brown hair, honey-gold streaks. Broad shoulders. She remembered the weight of his arm around her, the way he looked down at her when she slowed. He urged her onwards, telling her how special this place was to him, how special *she* was to him. It had warmed her then, made the irritation of her blisters less of a burden.

They had come to a clearing. She knew this clearing intimately, for it was where she now rotted beneath its surface. There had been an old shovel there already, half rusted. A blanket, spread on the ground. He had kissed her then, his tongue darting in between her lips when she opened them with a sigh. They had lain down, and she remembered the butterfly thrill in her stomach. His hand had crept up her bare leg, sliding underneath her to cup her closer to him, the other hand gliding up her arm to rest on her neck, gently, his thumb running back and forth over her jugular in a tender caress.

It wasn't long before the tenderness was gone and he was pressing hard, one broad hand across her throat, the other pinning her wrists. She had tried to escape, black stars exploding before her eyes, but he was too strong, and her body too weak.

This was how she had come to be in the forest.

She had been Abbey, and then she hadn't.

Around her physical body, the strands of mycelium tightened, as if giving her a comforting squeeze. The trees moaned with her; they did not condone killing for killing's sake, and furthermore, they loved her now.

The trees showed her three other sets of remains. The others tapped into the network as well, but their forms were only shells. They themselves had gone on to wherever they had left to go. They had never entered the forest, not in the way Abbey had. She could see them there beneath the surface of the soil, and she ran her "fingers" over them through the network of roots that had formed around them. They had been hollow since they died. Only she had remained behind.

Why now? she wondered. Why show Abbey all of this now?

The trees called again from farther out. She jumped into the network again, furious, and was there in the blink of an eye. Through the soil, she could feel him—the same vibrations the forest told her as when he had last visited. She did not have eyes, but she could see clearly.

It was definitely him. It was he who had brought her here, offering her unknowingly to the mycelium.

He was not alone. Someone smaller, someone gentler, walked alongside him.

More of Abbey came trickling back in. She had had long red hair. A loving father. A little sister named Lucy. Two cats—Bob and Bilbo. She had studied archaeology, and she preferred tea over coffee and a rainy day over a sunny one. She had a job in the museum giftshop and was about to start her master's degree.

Abbey waited for the lovers as they wandered off the path and into the deeper woods. Trees may not have ears or eyes, but they do have awareness. They communicated with her and each other, alternating their chemical signature for the breeze to catch, sending pulses of sugar and nutrients like Morse code messages through the mycelium. They could feel the vibrations through their roots, the cracking of small seedlings crushed underneath the duo's rhythmic footfalls.

The whole forest was ready and waiting for them, and so was she.

She flung herself up a tree, through the winding branches, and selected one, large and decaying. She stuck her "fingers" into it and gave several psychic tugs. With a great big crack, the bough broke and fell. She was back into the earth before it hit, smashing down onto the ground only two feet in front of the would-be lovers. She could feel them start, the panic of the smaller footsteps, the annoyed hitch of the larger. She could feel them move around the large branch, and she burst ahead again.

This time, the branch barely missed them. The smaller feet planted firmly and then turned around. The larger ones stayed still, and the trees told her that their voices were raised. After a moment, the smaller ones walked away quickly, jogging. The girl was leaving. There was a pause, and then Abbey's killer—Mark, she remembered his name now—followed the girl with grim and purposeful steps.

Abbey bolted again, and as he began to catch up, she brought a whole dead tree down in front of him. He stumbled backwards, but she was there again, pushing him deeper into the forest. She remembered Lucy's laugh, the tickle of her father's beard when he hugged her, the way Bilbo ate wet food like a fiend and always ended up coating his whiskers in fish paste. She wondered who was feeding her cats now, and the rage blossomed in her like a wildfire.

She drove Mark further on, herding him. Every time he strayed off the path she had set, something would fall or a tree would groan threateningly. Again and again, she snapped the branches in her fury. He was trying to flee. His footsteps pounded against the ground above her as she raced through the network, her will an engine that drove her faster than his feet as she knocked dead branches from their perches, close enough now that they brushed him as they fell, sending him spinning to the forest floor.

It didn't take long for her to bring him to where her body lay. His feet paused, his exhausted steps stumbling to a stop as he took in his familiar surroundings. Through the leaves of the trees she could taste his anger at being thwarted, his fear and his confusion. She would never know what he felt or thought in those moments, but that did not stop Abbey from imagining that it was as overwhelming as dying had been.

Pain. She remembered that now. Pain and fear. She had forgotten what those were, the very concepts of them. There wasn't pain or fear within the mycelium. There was just *being*. The memory of them flooded into her, an abrupt and horrible jolt as she recalled what they meant to a human. Despite the blessing that death had brought her, she remembered what it was like to live. While she did not necessarily want to live again, she still recognized the absence of life, and that *hurt*.

Within the space of a breath, she was beneath him. She sank into her body, simultaneously shrinking and growing herself to fit back within the confines of her old life. There was a groan as the stand of encircling trees sent her their nutrients through the roots, pumping energy into her as she tried to remember how a body worked. She was careful—her jaw moved for the first time in months, but her tongue had become coated in mushrooms, and she did not want to crush them, so she kept it open. She flexed her stiff fingers.

The forest shared willingly with her, as it always had. What was left of her became more mushroom than human, strands of stringy white replacing the missing muscles, massaging them with sugar. She moved slowly, so slowly at first, as the mycelium rebuilt her, sending tendrils running through what remained of her nervous system and replacing them. She inhabited them, her essence and existence stretching into places that consciousness had never been. She was more than just Abbey—she was Abbey a million, a billion times over, existing in every bit of her old body right down to the cellular level. Strung together by the network and fed by the trees, she found herself moving within the damp earth, uncurling among the roots. She reached up through the soil, the small hairs of the mycelium bursting forth through her skin like peach fuzz, shifting the dirt so it was as if her physical body were swimming through the soil.

Her rotted hand broke through from the surface and wrapped its hand around the ankle of her murderer. The fungi that held her together and pumped sucrose into her veins gave her strength, and she could feel him struggling. She brought her other hand up, gripping a tanned and muscled calf, and pulled herself up his body as if he were a rope to climb.

She could not see. Her eyes had long ago decayed, but his pulse thrummed beneath her fingertips, his muscles tensed, vibrations of his screams ripped through his body. The fine mycelium on the back of her neck rose and vibrated with him. She dove back into her grave, dragging him down with her.

The soil parted around them and then over their heads like a warm blanket. He choked on dirt as it poured down his throat. His heart stuttered and skipped in his chest before it stopped. The pounding of his blood in her ears faded to a gentle wave and then to a final stillness as it pooled within his veins. She waited within the network, but as the sounds of his life ebbed, he did not join her. He had also gone somewhere else. He would no longer send anyone else "somewhere else".

The rage that had driven her into her body again subsided, the intensity of her connection with her necrotic tissue beginning to fade. The trees offered her comfort in her exhaustion, the roots reaching towards her and wrapping around her in a primeval embrace while *his* body lay forgotten by them. The pain of remembering Abbey was a weight upon her being—the questions left unanswered, the pressure of a life unlived. She felt trapped inside her old flesh, trapped by her old life.

There was an internal pull then, a call that led out into the brilliant blue of the sky. It was sunshine and warmth, a lightness of being that sang to her and urged her to soar. She did not want to follow it. She could feel the tug of the mycelium leading her back into the ground, the filigreed grid of fungi waiting to embrace her again. The roots shifted; she heard the burrowing of the earthworms and the beetles, the thumping hearts of a family of mice. She could feel it all and longed to join it again. She would rather become one with the woods instead of heading into the sky that beckoned her. She sent a feeling of longing back into the ground, and the forest responded, the small hairs of the tree roots reaching for her, straining towards her with love and the promise of eternity. With that, she sank gratefully back into the mycelium, and forgot Abbey entirely.

VISITATION

Rose was just sitting down to her twice-weekly meal of donor meat when the intercom came to life. Her entire apartment had been wired so that no matter where she was, she could speak or be spoken to by her personal concierge without having to move. Usually, it was Rose requesting something or scheduling the booking of one of her many treatments, but this time, it was Gregory's pleasant chocolate-smooth voice interrupting her just as she was laying her napkin across her lap with a practiced flourish.

"Pardon the interruption, Madame Babineau, but your granddaughter is here for her appointment with you."

Annelise was early, that wretched child. Always rushing around with no concern for anyone else—or even herself. Visitations were usually set for after meals precisely for the protection of the guests.

"Would you like me to send her up?"

Rose's stomach growled, but she of all people knew she could keep her composure. She was a Babineau; little things like hunger did not prevent her from her social duties. Once, she had even met with a governor while suffering from a terrible stomach flu. He had been none the wiser. "Send

her up, please, Gregory," she said, not without a tinge of resentment that Gregory wisely did not react to.

"Yes, ma'am."

The intercom clicked off. Rose contemplated the lunch laid out before her and mentally steeled herself for an interaction with her least favourite (and only, following that horrible yachting accident off the coast of Brazil) relative.

She was sitting at her small dining room table for one, a lovely handmade lace tablecloth covering the immaculately polished walnut wood. Before her sat her tray, covered with a metal cloche. Two pieces of paper lay to the left and right of the formally arranged silverware. The left was a note from the chef in elaborate, curling script on beautiful textured cardstock. It detailed how today's meal had been tenderly massaged with a blend of truffle and rosemary oil before being garnished by thin slices of *foie gras* edged in edible gold foil. It was garnished with shaved truffles and Parmigiano. She would discard the truffles and cheese, of course, and see if her body would tolerate the goose liver. She had doubts she would enjoy it. Much to her chagrin, she'd become rather picky during the onset of her current condition.

On the right, the second paper was a simple funeral program, badly folded, with a blurry picture of a young, muscular man with golden curls smiling up at her. His name had been Justin. It was not the usual policy of the Berkham Wellness Spa and Village for the Freshly Deceased to include intimate information about her meals, but even before her change, she had always liked to know where her food had come from. Free-range, antibiotic-free, killed in a stress-free environment—she still held to the same principles as before despite her unique dietary restrictions. Furthermore, she found herself particularly enjoying any young men who joined her during her meals, and it was usually considered polite to have a basic understanding of someone before you sat down to dine with them.

With a longing glance backwards, she stood and made her way to the living room area of her quarters. They were quite large; she, in fact, inhabited the penthouse of the estate, courtesy of her family's extensive holdings in both land and factories, as well as her own smart investments. And, she admitted quietly to herself, her cutthroat business practices. One never got anywhere without a little blood spilled, especially if one was a Babineau.

Her rooms were opulently decorated—she'd brought her favourite furnishings from her coastal summer house in Greece to match the tastefully painted walls and marble flooring. It made her feel young again and like she was on a permanent vacation. Before an 18th-century French dresser, she pulled one drawer open with ease, revealing sets of elbow-length silk gloves in a variety of colours. She paused for a moment to consider and ultimately decided to go with white. She had always liked to present an immaculate appearance.

As she pulled them on, she took a minute to inspect her bite mark. She had only been at the spa for a few weeks, and they had yet to find an acceptable solution for the ragged, gaping dry wound on her wrist. Any donor skin or tendons would quickly wither and rot, and the few latex prosthetics she'd tried had not matched her new skin tone quite to her satisfaction. At her behest, Gregory sent out some e-mails to her contact list, and she had high hopes that a practical effects artist who was currently working on a large Hollywood horror franchise would solve that particular problem. But in the meantime, it was unseemly to look at or have exposed in the company of guests.

Once she slid the gloves on, she walked across the hall, heels clicking and echoing up to the grand ceiling to where a large, elaborated carved door stood—imported from Sri Lanka, and then retrofitted to look as elegant and natural as the rest of her home furnishings. It was much better than the rather plain wooden door that had so offended her when she first arrived.

The entrance to her penthouse was triple-reinforced. As she approached, the first wooden door unlocked courtesy of Gregory, operating it remotely. The second, a set of double-paned glass, parted. Finally, the steel blast containment doors swung open to reveal her parlour, where she entertained any guests. It was reminiscent of a Victorian gentleman's library—not her usual rococo aesthetic, but the spa found that the style worked well with containment protocols, as well as hiding the various things staff would need if something were to go wrong. Back when the spa had first opened for the ultra-wealthy upper-class who could afford the lifeevac helicopter within an hour of initial exposure, the astronomical rent, and regular "treatments", they had hand-delivered a beautiful information package to each member of the elite within a flight radius. At the time, she had thought it rather morbid and gauche but was glad she'd signed up for their list upon a second thought.

"Would you like me to go over the containment protocol with you, Madame Babineau?" Gregory asked.

"No, thank you, Gregory, I remember it from last time," Rose replied as she approached one of the plush, oversized armchairs. She sat herself down in one, unlatching the padded compartments on the top of each armrest, drawing out the gold-plated chains that would attach her to the chair. Within the headrest was a similar chain with an elegantly wrought collar. She attached the collar first before clasping the manacles around her wrists. She experimentally moved her arms and body so that Gregory could see via the cameras she was strapped in and had only had a limited circle of movement.

"Excellent, Madame Babineau. I shall send her in."

There was a hiss as another three doors opened on the other side of the parlour, and Rose carefully schooled her face into a neutral expression as her granddaughter sashayed in.

"Hey Grandmere," Annelise said, tossing her balayaged blonde hair over a slender, exposed shoulder. She pursed her pink lips into a critical shape as she took in Rose's captivity. Rose tensed, wondering if Annelise was going to comment on the waxy texture of her skin (she'd undergone a preservation treatment yesterday on top of her weekly formaldehyde-based mineral infusion) or her pallid complexion. She knew her cheeks were somewhat sunken (she had a consultation with a plastic surgeon next week to look into fillers and implants) and that her eyes had blackened (contacts were too damaging, she had learned, as she didn't produce tears anymore) and burned with the fire of un-death. But Annelise sat down without a word, one long leg crossing the other. She wore Black Louboutins. Rose thought privately to herself the heels were too high and the skirt too short, but Annelise had never cared to dress herself appropriately in deference to the Babineau name. It wasn't an argument worth having again.

"Hello dearest," Rose said as she reached for the steaming teapot on the side table that was within her range of movement. She could feel her throat starting to rasp as she spoke, and the tea made from the herbs used in Egypt's mummification processes would work wonders in both lubricating the muscle and maintaining the long-term integrity of the tissue. She poured it, explaining what was in it and apologizing she could not offer Annelise any. Annelise wrinkled her nose as the smell of the steam reached her.

"You know, I've heard of several sheiks and land barons who've undergone the process to become living mummies," Annelise said. "Which is just gross, in my opinion."

"They are lucky to have the opportunity," Rose responded patiently, "to become a piece of living history, instead of just incinerated." She thought for a second of the gardener who had originally bitten her. Rose's bodyguard detail had cut him down almost immediately; his remains turned to ash before her ride had even arrived. She didn't quite remember his name—something Bolivian? Guatemalan? He had been very new and from somewhere very poor. That was the only reason the virus occasionally even turned up in such a civilized country. It was practically unheard of in a developed nation.

"Whatever," Annelise said, unzipping her Hermes purse and digging through it in search of something. "Did you know they took Baxter when I got here?" Baxter was a miniature cocker spaniel that joined Annelise everywhere. Rose had always privately thought Baxter was the best part of Annelise's presence. Baxter had accompanied Annelise on her visit last week and had joined them in the parlour, but he had spent the entire time barking and growling at Rose, who had barely resisted the urge to snap her teeth back at him. He'd been entirely unhinged and had looked utterly delicious.

At the memory of the little dog, Rose's stomach growled again, and she couldn't help but grit her teeth a little bit. "To what do I owe the honour of a visit so soon after the first?" Annelise was never one for visiting her grandmother; the feelings of disdain were mutual between them. Rose hoped that this wouldn't take terribly long. She thought of Justin, waiting for her back in her rooms, and hoped he wouldn't spoil.

"Oh, yeah, right," Annelise said, drawing out the tube of lip gloss she'd been looking for. "I'm having you incinerated next week."

Rose gaped at her, manners temporarily forgotten.

"I didn't want to tell you," Annelise continued as she swiped her lips with shine and smacked them together, "but then when I asked everyone their opinion, they said that you should probably know just so you could enjoy your last week or whatever, that you were my grandmother, and then I felt guilty so...here I am."

"I don't quite know what you're thinking, dear," Rose said slowly. "But I am still *very* much conscious."

"I mean, yeah, but like, you're not actually *alive*, right?" Annelise said with a bit of a smirk, pointing her lip gloss at her grandmother in place of a finger.

"We are sitting, having a conversation right now." If Rose's heart could beat, it would be thudding in her chest.

Annelise snorted. "Yeah, in a zombie prison."

"It's a spa," Rose said stiffly. A red-hot heat spread through her veins, or what remained of them. "My brain is still perfectly intact." Granted, she had lost a few things before they could stabilize her, but nobody really needed Arabic, or Spanish, or basic multiplication. For the most part, she had remained herself.

"Anyway, I've been looking into it, and I talked to Mikey about it," Annelise continued. Rose sighed and closed her eyes. Michael was one of the lawyers on her legal team—the youngest and the brashest. *Youth.* "And Mikey said that you were technically, in a medical sense, dead, so we could probably start probate."

"Again, I am right here, and besides, I have a will."

"You didn't have an undead will. We found your living will and your, like, *dead*-dead will, but you never had an *undead* will made up, and that's kind of what is supposed to cover situations like this. And, like, this place is expensive. I saw the list of treatments you guys have, and if you're here for another few decades, there isn't going to be much left for me outside of my trust fund. I mean, you could go on *forever* with enough money. But because you don't have an undead will, it means I become your power of attorney or something. I dunno, it's all kind of messy still when it comes to zombieism. Mikey knows the details. And since you're undead and, like, a total menace, you become my problem, and according to the law, I can have you incinerated."

Rose's mind raced. What the vapid child was saying did, in a twisted way, make horrible sense. A loophole. If she were alive, bile would have risen in her throat. Her teeth and jaw began to ache, and her empty stomach twisted.

"Gregory," Rose said as calmly as she could. "Please call the Babineau Trust Legal Team." It might not be too late to get an undead will in order, though she would have to see if she still counted as firm in mind. She had a half of mind to eat her legal team anyway; they should have known she needed an undead will in the event she became infected. Now her fortune was about to be stolen out from over her cold dead body.

"Right away, Madame."

"Anyway, yeah, so I think we can get you incinerated next week, but I also have this show that I want to go to and during the cremation process they want me there, so it might get pushed to the next week," Annelise continued. "I dunno, we'll see. Depends on whether you have, like, any last requests or something."

"I can release a significant amount of funds to you," Rose said quickly, mind churning. "I do not think we need to resort to incineration. I am your grandmother, after all. We are Babineaus. Let us be civilized with one another."

Annelise looked at her in a way that was both condescending and pitying. "Okay, but the funds are practically already mine, and again, this place is *expensive*. I could pay for like an all-inclusive vacay in Bali for your daily fees. And I think a week or two is generous enough to make your peace with everything?" Annelise looked at her grandmother. "Or if you want, you can plan the funeral. I checked your dead-dead will, and you did have some instructions there. I could probably have someone carry them out."

Rose took a deep breath and massaged her temples. She technically didn't need to breathe, but she hoped it would calm her down. It didn't. Instead, the blind animal rage started to build. It was frightening in its intensity, but she thought she could manage one more appeal.

"Annelise, we are family, we are blood. We are Babineaus. We have not gotten this far without sticking together." Her hand hovered over the emergency button.

Annelise sighed, irritated. "I mean, yeah, we were family. But you don't have any blood anymore, soooo... As far as I and the banks are concerned, I'm the last Babineau." Annelise pulled a small compact mirror out of her purse and checked her lip gloss one final time before snapping it shut with a click. "I'm sorry, Grandmere, but it's just business."

Something dark and primal reared its head in Rose as she imagined the lick of the flames against her withered flesh, her granddaughter looking on impassively while Rose screamed and turned to ash. How dare she? How dare she do this to *her*, *Rose Babineau*? She'd helped build the empire this ungrateful brat was now trying to claim as her own. Damn it, and damn her. The last thread of her civility snapped and she stood abruptly.

"Madame Babineau, please be seated," Gregory's soothing voice came over the system. "Mademoiselle Babineau, please begin to make your way to the doors."

Rose ignored him and attempted to lunge at Annelise, who shrank away in horror.

"See, Grandmere? You aren't even human anymore. I'll see you at the crematorium," Annelise said snidely as she grabbed her purse and stepped out of Rose's range. "This is a good thing." She turned to make her way for the metal door, which began beeping its countdown to open.

Rose could not hold herself back any longer. Darkness rushed through her scrawny limbs, imbuing them with strength she'd never had, neither living nor dead. With a howling snarl, she lunged, the chains snapping, the manacles still hanging from her wrists like gold bangles. She could not break the collar holding her head, but with a hard enough yank, the part of the chair holding the chains splintered and broke, the headrest like an anchor flailing behind her.

Annelise shrieked as Rose's dainty gloved hands grabbed her from behind, yanking her by the hair and pulling her back, exposing her long and graceful neck. A klaxon alarm sounded, and Gregory's frantic yells rang over the intercom. The emergency response team was approaching and Rose knew she had only a few precious minutes left.

With a yowl, she sank her teeth into her granddaughter's neck.

Blood spurted down Rose's throat and down her front as Annelise's manicured fingers scrabbled weakly at Rose's face. Rose ripped a chunk of flesh from Annelise and swallowed it whole, her throat distending like a boa constrictor's. The two of them sank to the ground slowly, Rose's arms like a vice as she cradled her selfish granddaughter and devoured her.

When the emergency team finally surrounded her in their Kevlar uniforms, cattle prods and catch poles ready, their heavy helmets hid what surely must have been horrified faces. Rose was coming out of her red haze of her own accord. Her stomach was bloated and engorged as if she were heavily pregnant, and she was coated head to toe in red bits of flesh and viscera. Annelise herself was unrecognizable, her face gone, her body shredded, her torso cavernous and empty.

"There will be no need for that, gentlemen," Rose said languidly. "I am quite nearly myself again." She stood up, peeling off her sodden gloves, dropping them with wet splats onto the ground. Her hands gleamed white against the red of the room. She licked her lips and shuddered, eyes rolling back in her head. "I am finished." She stood unsteadily, off-balance, and she shakily made her way back to her rooms, the doors already opened as the Team had been quite prepared to either herd or drag her back to her palatial prison.

For the first time since her arrival, she felt satiated.

Before the doors closed behind her, she could hear one of the team radioing for the cleaning crew as another vomited into his helmet. It gave her an idea.

"Gregory," she said to the empty hall.

There was silence.

"Gregory."

"Yes, Madame," he responded finally, his voice quiet.

"I need you to bring up a video call with my legal team."

There was a pause. "Right now, Madame?"

Blood dripped from her, red rivulets running down to soak the carpet. It squished beneath her heels.

"Yes, please," she said pleasantly. "I have a few things I'd like to discuss with them. And do make sure the video on my end is on."

"Right away, Madame." There was an audible click as the intercom turned off.

Rose moved to the chair in front of the screen where she took her phone calls and leaned back with a satisfied smile. She ran her hands over her dress, smoothing out the worst of the wrinkles before she raised her fingers to her mouth, meticulously licking them clean one by one.

She was a Babineau, and it was time to remind people *exactly* what that meant.

THE CULL

THE PLUMES OF morning mist rose like ghosts through the trees, the sliver of red sun peeking over the horizon painting their edges a light pink. Jackson stood behind his truck, in the ruts of some old frosty tire tracks, looking across the barren farmer's field at the waiting woods. He heard two more pickup trucks crest the hill and pull over to park behind him. The rest of his group had arrived.

Jackson tapped out a cigarette from the box in his coat's breast pocket and lit it using his father's old Zippo lighter, taking a deep drag of it as he turned to watch Yusuf and Steve climb out of Yusuf's black Ford.

Harris stayed in the cab of his Toyota for a moment longer before he exited, reaching into his back seat and pulling out an old leather backpack and rifle. He slung both of them over the shoulders of his bright orange jacket and moseyed over to the other men.

"Colder than a witch's tit out here," Steve whined as the four of the men convened. He brushed his long blonde hair out of his eyes and scowled.

"It's November, what the fuck else do you expect?" Yusuf said, though his tone was good-natured.

Jackson grunted a greeting at both of them.

"Eloquent, as always," Harris said, shoving a woolen hat over his bald head. "So where are we going?"

"There are two permanent blinds in this area we have permission to use," Jackson said. "I figured we could split up into two groups for the hunt."

"And we don't need tags?" Yusuf confirmed, sipping from his steaming thermos cup.

Jackson shook his head. "I'm here in my official capacity as a conservation officer. There are several other groups heading out here to this area over the next two weeks. We're just the first, but I'm glad you all could join me."

"So we aren't here as friends?" Steve asked with a frown.

"I think right now we're considered volunteers," Yusuf said, reaching up to stroke his neatly trimmed beard. "I mean, we're all still friends, but Jack has to wear his work hat today." Jackson grunted at him again in the affirmative.

"Why the fuck are we culling the deer again?" Steve asked. Jackson could smell alcohol on his breath even from where he was standing. It was against the law to drink and hunt, but it didn't stop most hunters from cracking a few open when they were out in the woods, and it certainly hadn't stopped Steve from apparently thinking beer was a suitable breakfast food. Jackson knew he should be enforcing the law, but it would probably cause some strife in the group if he tried to send Steve home at that point. Besides, he needed all the warm bodies he could muster.

"There's a prion disease hitting the cervid populations hard," Harris replied when Jackson didn't. "Jackson needs us to kill a bunch of deer to slow the spread."

Jackson nodded, coming out of his thoughts. "It's called Chronic Wasting Disease. It's spreading like wildfire right now throughout the provinces and states. It's like Creutzfeldt-Jakob disease, but for deer."

Steve swore. "Are you saying I'll get mad cow disease? Lose my fucking mind? In that case, I'm out."

"It doesn't pass to humans, dipshit." Harris crinkled his nose, clearly already irritated with Steve. Jackson made a mental note not to pair the two men together.

"It doesn't transmit to humans, and we want to keep it that way," Jackson agreed. "It passes through close contact or bodily fluids. It stays in the soil and transmits easily between animals. It's spreading fast. We can only hope it doesn't end up evolving and making the leap to humans. Culling doesn't usually work with CWD, but recent tests on roadkill and deer hunted with tags here have shown the local deer population's incidence rate of CWD is a hundred and twenty-eight percent higher than in the next county over. No one knows why, but the local office thinks it's best if we try to lower the population to slow the spread. Zombie deer disease is no joke."

"What are we looking for? What happens if we shoot a deer that doesn't have it?" Harris asked, his dark eyes thoughtful.

"Deer that are skinny. Too skinny for having had all summer to fatten up for winter. They'll also just look...wrong. As for accidental shootings, it's hard to believe any deer in this area wouldn't be infected. Sometimes it takes a long time to show. Just shoot now, and we won't worry about it later." Jackson stubbed out his cigarette on the ground and put the butt in his coat pocket.

"What the fuck do you mean, they look wrong?" Steve said.

"Just wrong. You'll know it when you see it. Grab your shit, we're gonna drop Harris and Yusef off first." Jackson turned and started walking, not waiting for the other men, his mind whirring.

He could keep an eye on Steve if they were paired together, and that was probably for the best. Steve was a recent city transplant and new to the group of men, and nowhere near as experienced a hunter as the other three. In fact, he hadn't even been on Jackson's recruitment radar for the cull, but Steve had overheard his and Yusuf's conversation and asked to come. Yusuf, ever good-natured, had agreed to it before Jackson could even get a syllable out.

The sunrise stuttered to a stop as grey clouds rolled in, obscuring the light as the four men tramped silently across the field. Overhead, late migratory geese honked as they flew towards a warmer winter haven.

After a few minutes of walking into the woods, the group came to a largish clearing ringed by naked trees. On the opposite side from them was a small raised hut made of shining metal and crisp, grey tarp. It looked very new.

"Yusuf, Harris, this is your stop," Jackson said to them.

"This looks cushy," Yusuf said with a low whistle. "Way better than sitting up in a tree or in some flimsy tent. Might be a little warmer too."

Jackson took a moment to dig through his pack and then handed something to Harris.

"I have phone service." Harris took the radio anyway and tucked it into his back pocket.

Jackson shrugged. "Out here, that changes fairly often. Just keep it on and keep it close. Let us know if you see anything."

"Do you think we'll get anything?" Harris asked.

"The infected deer lose their sense of fear. I wouldn't be surprised if they walked right up to the blind, even if they know you're there. If you get one or more, we'll throw them in the back of the truck and take them in for testing and then incineration."

"I know we can't keep the meat, but I hope I get to keep any trophies I bag," Steve said with a touch of arrogance. Jackson didn't dignify it with an answer.

"Seems wrong to kill a sick animal and call it a trophy," Yusuf said with a roll of his eyes. "Culling a sick animal is not sport; we're doing it to protect the other herds before the disease can spread. That's just good wildlife management, and without that there wouldn't be any deer left to hunt."

Steve just shrugged. "Fine, you do you and I'll do me. But I want a rack of antlers for my living room."

"Could just pick up some sheds then," Harris muttered under his breath, but Steve ignored him.

Harris and Yusuf climbed into the hide and settled in. After a final wave, Jackson turned around and began hiking in another direction, Steve stumbling after him. They'd only gone about two kilometers when they came to an old tree bearing a dilapidated wooden treehouse, covered with mismatched plywood sheets and faded teenage graffiti. Thick chunks of wood were nailed to the tree in a crude ladder.

Steve looked at it with distaste. "Are you serious? I have to actually climb up into it like that? Why'd the other guys get the luxury one?"

"I thought you were an experienced hunter," Jackson said neutrally. "What, you've never been in a tree blind before?"

Steve blustered for a moment before he reluctantly climbed up, muttering the entire time. Jackson looked around at the area for a moment, taking in the rotting wet leaves and grey skies, before he followed up after him.

They sat there in silence for about half an hour, the cold air nipping at their exposed skin. Steve began to shift uncomfortably from where he sat on an overturned milk crate.

"I thought you said there would be deer," Steve said in a plaintive tone, just as Jackson heard a twig crack.

"Shut up," Jackson muttered to him. "Listen."

There was a sound as something came up from behind the blind. Leaves crunched underfoot, and a branch snapped as if something large had stumbled into a tree while moving towards them.

"Aw yes," Steve hissed, settling back down and hunching his shoulders. He placed his rifle up on the edge of the small window. Jackson frowned but didn't stop him. They sat quietly, waiting for the animal to reveal itself.

Stepping out from underneath the hide was one of the largest deer Jackson had ever seen in his twenty years of wildlife conservation. It still had its antlers, and what had once been a large and magnificent chest had become cavernous and sunken in. He could count its ribs through the fur. It got halfway across the clearing in a strange, shambling walk before it paused to look around.

From where they sat, Jackson could see the giant strings of saliva that hung from its mouth, and its head bobbed as its eye looked up at the blind, panting. Classic CWD.

"Jesus Christ, what an ugly fucker," Steve said, and then he took the shot.

The crack of the rifle echoed throughout the woods. The stag gave a surprisingly deep bellow and staggered from where the bullet struck his abdomen. Blood gushed from the wound, but the stag stayed on its feet and leapt out of the clearing, stumbling when it landed and rushing into the woods.

Jackson whirled towards Steve. "What the hell was that? That was a clean shot! I thought you said you could fuckin' hunt?"

Steve shrugged. "Hit it, didn't I? It'll crawl off and die. There will be another one, and that one I'll be sure to get."

"You can't just let it run off with a belly full of lead. That's inhumane," Jackson said. "You go put it out of its misery right now."

"It's already fucking dying," Steve protested. Jackson fixed him with a menacing glare. Steve refused to meet his eyes, looking away guiltily. Then after an awkward moment of silence: "Aw fuck. Guess if I'm gonna get that rack, I'm going to have to go fuckin fetch it anyway."

Jackson said nothing, just watched as Steve climbed down from the tree hide and crouched by where he had hit the deer. He stayed close to the ground, following the blood trail out of sight.

The radio crackled to life, Harris's voice startling him.

"Jackson? Are you there? Thought we heard a shot. Over."

"I'm here. Steve hit a stag but didn't kill it. He's going to finish it off. You seen anything?"

"There's a whole herd that just arrived. Like, there's twelve of them. They're all just standing there, staring at the blind."

"Do you want us to try to get them all?" Yusuf's voice was barely a whisper. "They're just...staring. Fuckin' creepy."

"What are you waiting for?" Jackson asked a little too harshly. Something was bothering him, but he couldn't put his finger on it. He frowned as he looked out at the empty woods, at the blood trail Steve had left to follow. It took him a moment, but he remembered that deer with CWD tended to go off on their own and travel without a herd. That an entire herd had banded together, especially one of notable size, seemed... wrong. "Go ahead and start shooting."

The radio was silent for a moment. "Sorry, mate," Yusuf said. "Just wanted to confirm." The radio went quiet and shots rang out from farther away in the woods.

In the space between the echoes, Jackson heard the scream.

It came from the opposite direction, from where Steve had disappeared after the stag. It was loud and shrill, full of panic.

The scream had barely faded away before Jackson was sliding down the trunk. He landed heavily on the forest floor, jarring his right hip, and he started off at a dead run down the path, slowing occasionally to make sure he was still following the trail of dripping blood and Steve's heavy boot prints.

The scream came again, ending in a painful howl that slowly faded. There was no third scream. Jackson crested a hill, skidding to a stop at the top of it as he looked down at the scene playing out before him in a small hollow shaped like a bowl.

Steve was there at the bottom of it, standing before the wounded stag. Its head was down, and it took a moment for Jackson to realize the stag's antlers were impaled through Steve's chest, the points bursting outwards through his back. The checkered flannel of his shirt was marked by a slowly growing red stain. There was a groan, and the stag stepped back, yanking his antlers out of Steve with a sickening squelch. Unsupported, Steve slid slowly to the ground.

As the stag stared up at the sky with blank, filmy eyes, it dawned on Jackson that he'd left his gun back at the hide. He'd grabbed the first-aid kit instead. Jackson unzipped his jacket and flapped it open and began to holler, trying to make himself as large as he could, hoping the deer would flee and he could get to Steve, who was moaning softly.

The stag paid him no mind, instead leaning down its long, arched neck to stick its muzzle into Steve's neck, the large black nose snuffling him. Steve weakly lifted a hand and attempted to bat the stag away, but it pushed its muzzle harder into the throat of Steve's shirt. There was a horrifying crunch and a wet tearing noise before the stag raised his head. Long strips of skin and flesh and what suspiciously looked like the grey muscle of vocal cords hung from between the stag's blunt teeth. The deer began to chew, slurping up the stringy flesh as if it were spaghetti. At its feet, there was a horrible burbling noise, a final weak convulsion, and then the moaning stopped and Steve was still.

The contents of Jackson's stomach rushed up his throat and flooded his mouth as the deer chewed on its mouthful of flesh as if it were cud.

Turning his head, he spat some coffee-flavored vomit onto the ground as he struggled to get his emotions under control. He took a deep breath. He spotted Steve's rifle at the bottom of the hill, lying a dozen feet from the deer and the dead man.

The stag finished chewing and audibly swallowed before it lowered its head to take another chunk of the meat that had recently been Steve. Jackson knew that, very rarely, and often on islands or remote areas, deer became opportunistic omnivores, eating small frogs, invertebrates, or the occasional bird, to get essential and missing nutrients, but for a deer to eat a person? That was unheard of.

Jackson moved down the steep hill, careful not to slip. Sweat trickled down the back of his neck as he crept towards the rifle, and he resisted the urge to wipe it away. The stag continued to ignore him in favour of its unconventional meal. When he was only a few feet away, the stag looked up, blood dripping from its hairy lips as it noticed Jackson for the first time. It snorted and stamped its hoof at him.

Jackson stared into those dull and fevered eyes, and made a leap for the gun, his hand closing around the barrel.

The stag bellowed and charged. Jackson swung the rifle smoothly up to his shoulder and shot, and the beast stumbled and fell, sliding across the slick rotting leaves to gently bump against Jackson's boots. Its eye was gone, and the wet cavity of where it had been now stared sightlessly up at the sky.

He shot it again between the eyes just to make sure it was dead, and then he ran to Steve's side.

Steve was also dead; there was no doubt about it. Not only had he been impaled through several vital organs, more than half his throat and an entire cheek were gone, the evidence of the agony and shock of his death still plainly written across his features.

Steve was not a small man. There was no way Jackson would be able to get his body back to the truck on his own, especially not over such uneven terrain and with the potential threat of more deer looming. Jackson had just finished making the executive decision to mark the location and head back for help when he felt eyes on him. Cold fear flooded through him, and when he looked up, three does were watching him from the top of the other side of the hollow.

They moved slowly towards him, picking their way down the hill, their slender legs lifting high like ballerinas. One of them had a seized neck, the muscles having atrophied, her head lying completely sideways. All three of them looked ragged and unkempt, reminding Jackson of one of his daughter's well-loved stuffed animals. Like the stag, long strings of drool trailed from their mouths. Jackson had never seen such advanced infections as these. Something about the virus had drastically changed, and now these woods were not safe to be in. He needed to get back to the other men.

He carefully backed away from Steve's body, slowly making his way up a shallower and more circuitous route as the deer approached.

The three does stopped their advancement as they came to the remains, bending their heads down to the corpse. They began to feast, the cloth ripping loudly as they tore into him. When he reached the top of the hill, Jackson turned and ran, leaving behind the sounds of Steve being devoured.

It was only another minute or two to the hide, and as he clambered up into the safety of it, he could hear the radio blaring and crackling. Gunshots still rang out to the East, more measured now.

"JACKSON. STEVE. COME IN." Yusuf's panicked voice crackled. "Harris! They aren't answering!"

Jackson grabbed his rifle, slung it over the shoulder still carrying Steve's. "It's me. I'm here."

"Jackson, there's something fucking weird going on. There's twenty, thirty deer here. They're all infected. Some of them are just skin and bones. We keep shooting, but they take a while to go down. It's like they can't feel pain."

"Their brains are too far gone," Harris swore, his voice fainter in the background.

"They're eating the dead ones. They keep looking up at us—they know we're in the hide. A few of them have rammed the support struts. I don't want to think about what would happen if they gave way. We need you and Steve to come get us the fuck out of here."

Jackson paused before he responded. "Steve's dead. I'm on my way." He grabbed his pack and exited the hide.

"What do you mean, Steve's dead?" Yusuf's voice was incredulous. "We just saw you!"

"Steve's dead. The stag got him."

Yusuf swore. "That's not good."

"Goes without fuckin' saying!" Harris said in the background.

"You're right," Jackson said. "This isn't good. In fact, I'd say it's really fucking bad. We're getting out of here. I'm coming to you, and then we'll get you out of the hide and make a break for it."

"We're already almost out of bullets," Harris said. "It's like a siege over here. It's a fucking horde of zombie deer."

Jackson's shoulders sagged for a moment. "I'm not far."

"Walk softly, keep your big stick ready," Harris said. The echoing shots grew louder as Jackson jogged towards them. "If you can skirt around the clearing and provide cover fire, we can make a run for trucks."

Anxiety sat like a stone in the pit of Jackson's stomach. "Okay, but be careful. The stag impaled Steve, and then it ate him."

There was a static-filled silence.

"I'm sorry, can you repeat that?" Yusuf said.

"It ate him. I killed it, but there are three doe that were...congregating around Steve as I left him."

"It fucking ate him. Lovely. Just lovely. Jack, mate, next time you ask for a favour, you can go fuck yourself. I'm never going hunting with you again."

"Roger that," Jackson replied. "I'm going silent now. I'll press the transmission button when I'm in a position to cover you guys while you escape."

"Good luck," Yusuf said solemnly, and then Jackson was alone again.

He crept for the last kilometer. Here and there a gunshot rang out when a deer got too close to the hide, but it was clear the other men were conserving what little ammo they had left. He tried to give the clearing as wide a berth as possible as he made his way towards a good position.

Twice he had to drop to the ground when he heard light footsteps moving toward Harris and Yusuf. The deer seemed to be drawn to the chaos and the iron tang of blood that now hung thick in the air. Jackson army-crawled the final hundred metres. He crouched beneath the low-slung branches of an evergreen and surveyed the carnage that had filled the clearing where the hide was.

It was a slaughter. At least two dozen deer lay in the clearing in a fifty-foot radius around the hide. The trees were splintered, oozing sap from where many panicked shots had gone astray. Six strange-looking deer remained, picking their way through the corpses of their brethren. They stopped now and then to graze on the dead and the dying, their muzzles caked in wet crimson.

When they had first planned to come out here, Jackson had hoped to kill one deer per man. This was far beyond anything Jackson could have expected. The massacre that occurred here was monumental, and still the deer kept coming, walking out of the forest and onto the battleground to feast on their fallen brothers and sisters.

A bullet whizzed overhead and hit a nearby tree. Jackson pressed his body closer to the ground. To get hit by friendly fire would just be icing on the cake. He brought the radio up to his face, his lips brushing against it as he spoke.

"Stop shooting, assholes, you nearly hit me. I'm here," he whispered.

There was no answer, but he could see movement in the windows of the deer hide, and the barrel of Harris's gun disappeared from where it had been peeking out of the window.

Jackson moved into a kneeling position, absurdly grateful for all those weekends he spent with his father during hunting season and the skills they had instilled in him. He saw Yusuf wave through the door of the hide, and that's when Jackson started shooting.

He picked off two in the time it took for the men to jump down and start running. Their movement drew the deer to them, and they started giving chase in fevered stumbles, their usual grace and speed hampered by the prions slowly devouring their brains. More deer came out of the woods in halting steps, drooling and staring before they joined in the stampede across the clearing.

Jackson did his best to pick them off, but it wasn't long before he too was out of ammo. He wouldn't have time to reload. He tossed his rifle aside as the other men continued running towards him, Yusuf quickly outstripping Harris's short round legs.

"I'm out! I'm out!" Jackson screamed, urging them on as he stood and prepared to run with them. Yusuf shot past him, and as Jackson turned to follow, he saw what happened next from the corner of his eye.

Harris tripped over the splayed legs of a stag missing half of its head and went down, the herd of deer leaping after him. Within seconds, three deer—two does and a stag with only one antler—were on him and began to trample him, pounding their hooves down while he screamed. Red splatter flew up to coat their tawny chests as they turned his body into a sticky pulp beneath them.

Jackson didn't hesitate. He took off after Yusuf. The two men ran for the trucks, their legs churning and their lungs burning. Each breath was agony, and each step came with the fear that they might trip and fall as well. Behind them, something crashed through the underbrush at their heels, spurring them on.

As they came to the treeline bordering the farmer's field where they had parked, Yusuf reached into his pocket, slowing down slightly as he fumbled for and clicked his key fob. His truck beeped, and the two of them tore across the field. Yusuf ran around the car, and Jackson yanked open the passenger door and slid in. He had only just closed it when the stag with one antler rammed into the side of the door, denting it. One of its forelegs snapped and down it went, its eyes rolling wildly. Yusuf slammed his own door shut and jammed the key into the ignition.

Jackson stared out at the stag. Its large brown eyes were devoid of any real thought. He saw only aggression as it looked back at him, baring its teeth at him as he buckled himself in.

Yusuf started sobbing quietly, his shoulders shaking as he gunned the engine. As he peeled away and picked up speed, an emaciated deer jumped into the road, sliding across the hood of the truck and crashing straight through the windshield. Jackson screamed. Yusuf yanked the steering wheel. The truck careened off the road and was airborne for a moment before it landed, the momentum causing it to spin. The airbags deployed, knocking hard against Jackson's teeth and rattling his skull as the truck rolled over and over until it smashed against a tree right-side up and rocked to a standstill with a final violent lurch.

Inside the cab, Jackson's sight was blurry, his head throbbing and his body racked with pain. He was sure he had a concussion and that one of his arms was fractured.

The now-dead deer was between him and the steering wheel, its legs jutting out at awkward angles. Its hoof had sliced open Jackson's left cheekbone, and hot blood dripped down his face to puddle on his lap. He leaned against the airbag for a moment, his chest on fire, trying not to vomit. He could already feel the soft-tissue damage from where the seat belt had crushed him.

"Yusuf," he groaned. "Are you okay?"

There was no answer.

He lifted his head to look across the cab. The driver's seat was empty.

Yusuf had not been buckled in. When the deer had gone through the windshield and he had yanked to the side, he had also gone through the windshield, though in the opposite direction. He lay in a broken, flattened heap at the side of the road, completely still.

Jackson groaned and tried to undo his seatbelt. It was jammed. His fingers reached for the hunting knife still strapped to his leg. He sawed through the fabric, having to stop halfway through when dizziness nearly made him pass out.

The crumpled passenger door was also stuck when he tried to open it. He crawled across the dead deer, his hands gripping its matted fur to help drag himself across. He pushed open the driver's side door and slid out, taking a moment to vomit into the mud before he crawled to Yusuf's side and turned him over.

Yusuf's face was gone. His gentle features had been erased, road grit and forest debris coating the exposed muscle and bone. His limbs were at awkward angles to his body, and when Jackson placed two fingers against Yusuf's neck, he wasn't surprised to find he didn't have a pulse.

Jackson tried to stand, and he managed it, but he found that he couldn't take a step. From the woods, a deer bellowed. Jackson stood there, swaying on the side of the road, and stared out at the fields and forest, a hollow numbness spreading through his chest. His friends were dead. He was as good as dead. He fell to his knees next to what remained of Yusuf and closed his eyes.

He was sitting like that, eyes closed and waiting for death, when a white minivan came roaring up the road and pulled over, honking the whole time. The front doors swung open and disgorged a bald man and a curvy redhead out onto the side of the road.

"Oh my god," the woman said as she ran to Jackson to steady him. Her eyes were wide, and her lip began to quiver. The man slowed to a stop and stared numbly at Yusuf.

"We have to get out of here," Jackson said to them, his voice hoarse. "Please, we need to leave." The effort of speaking made the pounding in his head harder, and he half-collapsed into the woman's arms.

"We need to call an ambulance," the man said, blinking slowly. He was in shock.

"Call in the car," Jackson groaned. "Just drive."

"We can't do that," the man said. "This is the scene of an accident, we can't just leave."

"I am an officer, and I am telling you we *need to leave right now*," Jackson roared. "We aren't safe here!" He turned his head and threw up long strings of bile tinged with blood. His heaving caused his cracked ribs to protest, and he moaned as he wiped the back of his hand across his mouth.

The man and the woman looked at each other for a long moment, hesitation and fear warring in their eyes before each of them grabbed one of Jackson's arms and half-carried, half-dragged him over to the minivan. The woman slid the door open, and the two of them helped Jackson into one of the middle seats.

Two small children sat in the back row, gaping at the bloody man in their vehicle.

"It's going to be okay," the woman said. Jackson didn't know if she was speaking to him or the children.

He groggily managed to click in the seatbelt before his head began to sag. The man and the woman slammed the doors, and as the man pulled away, the woman was already on the phone with 911, speaking in a high-pitched and panicked voice.

Jackson fought unconsciousness, his whole body vibrating with pain, exhaustion, and grief. Something inside him told him to look back, and he craned his head to look over the heads of the two terrified children and out the back windshield.

A single deer stood in the middle of the road and stared after them as they drove away. The last thing Jackson saw as the minivan crested a hill was the long and ragged sliver of Harris's bright orange jacket hanging from between its bloodied teeth, and then it was gone.

PUP

SHE NEVER DID decide whether the specter of the grim that had dogged her footprints from childhood was a comfort or a curse. Its canine presence at her side was the only commonality between the tragedies that haunted her. Whether the dog was the cause of the affliction or merely a bystander offering what comfort it could give during her tumultuous life was unknown; all Suzanne knew was that it would be there during the lowest of her lows, and she didn't have a choice in it.

The first of the four times the dog entered her life was on her eighth birthday as she came home from school, only four or five blocks away from the small yellow brick house where she lived alone with her mom. She swung her new Rainbow Brite lunchbox, slapping it against her thigh where it left a stinging red mark. She was proud—*so proud*—of it, and that today she was able to walk all the way home by herself today without her mother's hand clutching her own. Around her, other groups of children and parents walked with her, so she was not truly alone, but regardless of that, she felt very grown-up. When Suze turned the corner onto her street, she could see her mother waiting at the end of her driveway a block away, waving at her.

One of her knee-high socks had fallen and bunched around her left ankle. She knelt down on the sidewalk, small bits of gravel stinging her knee as she tried to fix it. She couldn't get it to stay up. The elastic was broken. She remembered at the time being worried her mother might be upset, since the socks were new, opened just that morning at the breakfast table. She was distracted from her worries by a flash of fur beneath an evergreen bush beside the battered front porch of the house she'd stopped in front of.

The house itself was old and dilapidated, with a sagging red roof and shutters covered in peeling blue paint. The man who had been living there had died last week. Her mother had gone over to speak to a paramedic standing next to his silent ambulance. Suze had asked her mom about it, about the man who had lived and died there. Her mother had only said that he had been very old and very sad, and then had told her not to ask questions about it and to go brush her teeth.

Suze stood up, putting her plastic lunchbox gingerly on the grass. There was another flash of fur, and she walked across the lawn towards the house. A small dog, very small, so small it barely reached her prepubescent knee, trotted out from behind the bush. It had long white fur that was matted and hung in dreads as well as a flat face and a black nose. It wore a faded blue collar, and from it dangled a small and tarnished brass mirror. The dog's eyes were large and black and framed by ragged bangs.

The girl and the dog regarded one another. Suze knelt down and extended her hand slowly, like her mom had shown her how to do. The dog walked over, sniffed it, and licked it once. She held her breath.

"Suze!" Her mother called from down the street, a note of panic in her voice. "Suze!"

Suze stood up and took a few steps backwards. The dog watched her with its dark eyes.

"Bye," Suze said, and she grabbed her lunchbox and began walking again. Behind her, she heard the scrabble of small claws against the sidewalk. She turned around, and the dog that had been following her stopped and looked at her.

"I'm not sure you should do that," Suze said. "But it is my birthday, so maybe Mum won't mind."

She started walking again, and the dog continued to follow her. She walked down her street and up her driveway and climbed the concrete stairs to her small house. Her mom now stood in the doorway waiting for her and smiled, kneeling down to give her a big hug.

"Hey there, birthday girl," her mother said, kissing Suze on the tip of her nose. "How was your day?"

Suze launched into a ramble about her birthday. Mrs. Vaya had brought her a chocolate cupcake with rainbow sprinkles, and the whole class had sung her happy birthday. Her mother smiled and nodded as she ushered her daughter inside. Suze told her everything that had happened at recess, and how Brian Foster had told her that her freckles were ugly but had then kissed her on the cheek and run away. The dog followed eagerly inside, claws clicking against the stained linoleum.

Her mother made her mac and cheese with chopped-up hotdogs in it, and Suze had arranged the hotdogs so that they smiled back at her from a yellow face. The dog stayed under the table, pressing its cold nose against Suze's dangling calf. Her mother had also made a pie with some old apples, and Suze blew out the candles on it. She had already had a cupcake that day, so she didn't mind that it was a birthday pie and not a cake. She fed a piece of pie crust to the dog. Later, she and Mum watched *Cinderella* on VHS. The dog sat near the door and observed, its wagging tail brushing the floor with a comforting swish. She had sat curled up on her mother's legs and wrapped up in the pink comforter from off of her bed, and thought to herself that it was a good birthday. She was happy. She fell asleep there on the couch, a smile on her face.

Not once did her mother ever mention the dog.

It was ten minutes past the end of Suze's birthday when the doorbell rang, waking her from her spot on the couch where her mother had let her sleep. The doorbell rang again, and then heavy fists pounded against the door. Suze looked up from the couch as her mother tip-toed silently to the front window, peered through the ratty curtains, and began to tremble.

"Cream puffs." Mother whispered the code word known only between the two of them. Suze was instantly awake. "Suzanne, Cream puffs."

Without a sound, Suze ran to the home phone and grabbed it from its charger. She dashed into the bathroom, the dog following eagerly. She locked the door, and then locked the three deadbolts Mother had added immediately after moving into the old house. With chubby fingers, she sat on the toilet and punched in 911 as she heard her mother open the front window a crack and speak out into the night air.

"This is 911, what's your emergency?"

"My dad is trying to get into the house, and he's not supposed to be."

"Where's my daughter?" a slurred voice roared from the front porch. "Thought you could keep me from her on her birthday?"

"Vince, you're not supposed to be here. There's a restraining order. Go away." Mother's voice was a hoarse whisper that Suze could barely hear.

"Okay, how old are you, sweetie?"

"I'm eight. He's not supposed to be here. He's going to hurt us."

"Shut up, bitch, I wanna say Happy Birthday to my little girl. Suzanne? Suzanne, where are you?!"

"You can't see her, Vince. Last year, you gave her a broken arm on her birthday."

"I can give her whatever the fuck I want. I'm her father. I brought a doll, see? A *doll*! Now out of my fucking way, I'm coming in."

She heard the front door splinter and then slam against the wall of the cramped vestibule. Mother shouted angrily. Her father, definitely inside the house now, grunted. There was a heavy thud, followed by Mother sobbing and pleading for him to stop. Suze began crying into the phone as the lady on the line wrested the address through her gulping sobs.

"Stay on the line, sweetie, someone's coming for you, someone's coming for you, I promise."

Her father was still yelling, and Mother was now silent. The thudding sound continued. "I'm coming for you, Suzanne, I'm coming for you! You can't hide from Dad!"

The dog remained silent as Suze cleared out the cupboard under the sink, still crying into the phone. She climbed into it, and the small white dog followed. She huddled under there, listening to her father scream. The thudding stopped, and the sound of smashing furniture followed him as he stormed through the house like a clumsy predator.

Suze pushed herself as hard as she could against the back wall, her knees awkwardly jammed into the old lead piping, trying not to sob audibly.

"Someone's coming for you, Suzanne," the operator said reassuringly.

"I'm coming for you, Suzanne!"

The dog stared at her with its fathomless eyes. She started whimpering, and the dog hunched closer to her, still staring. Father roared outside the bathroom door, and it began to rattle. The dog moved closer, leaning against her. She sunk her fingers into its fur, gripping it and taking comfort from its presence.

Suddenly, there were strange voices and more yelling. Father bellowed, and there was a large bang and a wet noise and the bathroom door shook again, and now it exploded inwards and there were splinters everywhere and Suze was crying and strange arms were around her, soothing, while a voice murmured over and over again, and she saw her father and mother both lying in shimmering dark pools and she was being lifted into an ambulance and there were bright lights and the strange voice kept speaking so calmly and she asked about the dog and her mother, increasingly hysterical, and she was told that no dog was found, there is no dog, and then there was a prick in her arm and the push of a needle and...

Then there was nothing.

The second of the four times Suze saw the dog, she didn't recognize it at first. It wasn't until *after* everything happened that she remembered.

Suze now lived with her maternal grandmother in a different house in a different city and went to a different school there, where nobody knew about her parents or the newspaper headlines. She liked it that way. Suze was twelve—older and much wiser than she ought to be. There were many things she knew about that she didn't speak of, and she and her grandmother hardly ever brought up her parents.

Suze was quiet at school, but talented. Her elderly teacher adored the tiny child with big dark eyes who sat silently in the middle of the classroom. Suze had a few friends, but the twins were her best friends. They were everything Suze wasn't: loud, outgoing, gregarious. They had seen somber little Suze on her first day, sitting alone on a playground bench, and they immediately attached themselves to her. She didn't talk much around them. She didn't have to; they loved to talk so much, and Suze loved to listen.

The twins didn't look alike. Gregory was stocky, snub-nosed, and blonde. Lucia was heavily freckled, ginger-haired, and all knobby elbows and knees. The only similarity between the two of them was their loud speech and hazel eyes. They were popular on the playground, but everywhere they went, they insisted Suze follow.

"I don't think homework on weekends should be legal," Greg complained one April afternoon as they walked home from school. Suze's grandmother had given her permission to have dinner with the twins. Their mother was making lasagna, Suze's favourite.

"We need homework," Lucia retorted. "That way we can get smart. Or at least, the people who do their homework can get smart," she snarked across the sidewalk. Greg tried to shove her into the empty road. They tussled for a moment before Lucia won, and they continued making their way home.

"Suze? What do you think? About homework, that is," Gregory asked.

"I think it's good for discipline," Suze said distractedly. Something across the street had caught the corner of her eye, a small white shape that woke something in her subconscious.

"You're both such keeners," Greg sniffed. They walked in silence for a few moments. Suze kept looking back and lingering, trying to spot whatever-it-was she thought she had seen.

"What are you looking at?" Lucia asked, scratching her sunburnt nose. She had a tendency to burn, even in the pale April light.

"I thought I saw a dog," Suze replied.

"A dog is nothing special," Greg replied. "We used to have a dog at home." The twins' mutt, Snoopy, had passed away a few months ago.

"I know," said Suze, but her instincts told her differently. She looked back again, and that's when she saw a small, white, and matted dog staring back at her from the spot on a muddy lawn where it now lay. It got up when she looked at it. Its eyes were dark pits. Suze shivered. There was something familiar about the dog that unnerved her, even as it wagged its small tail.

"Don't you see it?" Suze asked her friends.

Lucia glanced back. "Nope. Now let's get moving."

The dog followed them closely for the remaining blocks. Suze couldn't shake her feeling. Every time she glanced back, the dog was closer. Lucia and Greg continued to chatter at each other. Suze didn't bring the subject of the dog up, even when it caught up and began to trot right next to her, its fur brushing against her jeans. The trio of children paused at a crosswalk, and the dog took the opportunity to jump up and lick Suze's hand. Its tongue was cold and slick, and she rubbed her hand dry against her pants, her stomach churning.

When they reached the twins' house, the dog entered with them. The twins' mother had laid out a small platter of ginger-molasses cookies and three glasses of milk on their cramped table shoved in the corner of the kitchen. Suze slid into the seat furthest away, next to the fridge. She could feel the hum of the refrigerator and laid her cheek against its cool side. The dog went under the table and panted at her feet.

"What are three things you learned today?" the twins' mother asked her customary question to the three of them as she laid down a final layer of pasta on the lasagna. She grabbed a ladle from a simmering pot of tomato sauce and poured it over the top.

"I learned that Mesopotamia is where mankind originated from," Lucia said proudly.

"That is a good thing to know," her mother said. She grabbed a glass bowl full of shredded cheese and began sprinkling it on top of the sauced noodles. "If you know where you came from, it's easier to know where you're going."

"I learned that a whale's penis is eight feet long," Greg crowed. Lucia groaned, and their mother stifled a chuckle.

"Not the most enlightening of facts," she said, "but at least you're learning." She finished with the cheese and retrieved her oven mitts. "And what about you, Suze?" she prompted as she crouched down and opened the oven door.

Suze opened her mouth to reply, and that's when the oven exploded.

Later, the firefighters said it was her proximity to the dingy yellow refrigerator that saved her. That, and her own quick thinking. She had slid out from underneath the scorched table and ran for the door, through the billowing smoke that burned her lungs and made her eyes water, past the smoldering corpse that was the twin's mother, and past the infernos that were her best friends. Lucia's hair, sliding off from her skull, Gregory's burning hands beating at his flaming clothing. And their eyes—black pits, staring at her just like the dog that now sat unbothered and unharmed in the corner of the kitchen as it watched the horror unfold. Lucia's and Gregory's mouths had been open, and they had been screaming, screaming loud and harsh over the crackling flames. The wallpaper began peeling away from the walls from the heat.

She was still there, wrapped in a blanket in her grandmother's arms, when the fire in the house was finally extinguished. Suze's arms were burned, but not badly. The scars would fade in a few years. The firefighters carried out one small and blackened figure on a stretcher. She never found out whether it was Greg or Lucia. She didn't want to know, never wanted to know. She only remembered the crispy blackened texture of its skin, and the sound the zipper made as it closed up over the withered face with its lips pulled back in a burnt grimace. The teeth were white and gleamed in that terrible mouth.

She didn't tell her grandmother about the dog, or the way it appeared to her in her nightmares, still sitting in the corner of that burning kitchen. Even in her dreams, she always wondered if the dog's eyes were just reflecting the flames or if they held hellfire of their own. Those eyes pinned her there, in among the smoky wreckage and steaming shrapnel. The dog would open its mouth and, like a stuck record player, her friends' mother's voice would come spilling out, asking the same question over and over and over again until she would wake gasping and drenched in sweat.

"And what about you, Suze?"

The dog was a mainstay in her nightmares from then on out, but it would be another thirteen years before she would see it again. Her grandmother had been moved to a facility after a bad fall, and Suze now lived with her boyfriend Jonah in a small walk-up apartment downtown. It wasn't the best of areas, but it wasn't the worst of areas. She worked as a junior editor at a video production company. The hours were long and the pay minimal, but she liked it well enough. Her only complaint was that sitting hunched over a keyboard for eight hours at a time made her back hurt. To combat that, she would often go for an evening walk with Jonah. They had a regular route mapped out down to the pipeline trail near them, a long and winding path that cut through the whole city, crossing parkland, back alleyways, and scenic views, and walked for about an hour.

Jonah was a nice man, and Suze sometimes entertained the thought that the two of them might get married someday. He hadn't really shown any inclination towards marriage, but he always made sure that Suze felt loved. He knew about those two episodes in Suze's childhood and was adequately supportive, but she had never told him about the dog.

She never told *anyone* about the dog.

So one night while she was out walking with Jonah and saw a flash of white out of the corner of her eyes, she refused to follow the urge to look. Her heart sped up, and she walked a little faster, sour bile filling her mouth.

"Slow down, Suzanne," Jonah said as he grabbed her by the hand. "You'd think you didn't want to take in the fall foliage."

The bright reds and yellows of the autumn leaves at that moment only reminded her of a burning kitchen and the screams of her childhood friends.

"I'm just tired," she said. "I'm a little ready to go home, maybe watch a movie."

He smiled down at her. His brown eyes had the perfect crinkles at the corners.

"Just tired," she said again. "Promise."

Something rustled in the leaves behind them.

She and Jonah continued their walk, but Suze kept her eye on the trail. In about twelve hundred meters, she knew that they would come to one of the trail exits. They would climb the hill that led to the main road. They would walk along the sidewalk, and in eight minutes they would be home. She would lock the front door and shutter the blinds. In the back of her mind, she could hear the crackle of flames, the angry shouting of her father, the sound of her grandmother crying.

Whatever was behind her sped up, the rustle of the leaves on the ground becoming more insistent, trying to encourage her to look back. Suze refused.

"Let's get to the road," she said hoarsely. "And call a taxi."

Jonah glanced at her with surprise. "It's not a far walk from the trailhead."

"I know, I'm just really tired," she insisted. The path was clearer now with fewer leaves to wade through, and she could hear small, fast footprints across the gravel. She knew Jonah couldn't hear it, otherwise he would have turned around. Her heart sped up as the sound of panting reached her ears.

"Are you sure you're okay?" Jonah raised his hand and touched her forehead with the back of it. "You're flushed, but you don't feel feverish."

She *felt* like she had a fever. Her heart pounded like a drum. She could feel each individual pulse in her face. She was shaking.

"Please, can we just call a cab?"

He stared at her, concerned, and stopped. She pulled on his hand, but he didn't move.

"Please, just let's keep going. Don't stop moving," she said, ripping her hand out of his and continuing walking. She pulled ahead of him and took the turn.

It was to breathe. She could hear Jonah behind her, laboring to get up the hill, and behind that she could hear the panting of a very small dog trying to keep up. She started sprinting up the hill and barely stopped herself from skidding into the busy road when she reached the top. Behind her, Jonah shouted.

"Suzanne! Wait!"

There was a crosswalk nearby. She barely caught the tail end of the crossing signal and ran across the road. Her eyes stung, her chest heaved. Just as the light turned green, she turned around.

Jonah wasn't as lucky when he came to the top. He tried to stop himself. The worry in his eyes turned to panic as he crested the hill and realized he was running right into the oncoming traffic. He tried to brake, hands out in front of him as if to brace for a fall. And he did fall as he tripped over the curb, twisting his body so his shoulder hit the pavement and bounced a little bit. His eyes widened as he hit the ground, looked into hers for a quarter of a second as they understood what was about to happen. Suze saw all of this as if it were in slow-motion.

She also saw the bus approaching. Time sped up again, and then there was noise. So much noise. The bus honked. Its brakes screamed. Then a thud and a wet skid, and a red slab of meat that rolled out from underneath the bus and then under the wheels of a grey Honda. Someone was yelling, people were flooding off the bus as the ragdoll that had been her boyfriend was tossed and turned beneath the wheels of multiple vehicles. Suze was reminded of a car stuck along a muddy country road—the whirring liquid thrown up in chunks and spurts, the angry wheels and revving engine. Somebody was screaming.

On the other side of the road, a small white head followed by a body came trotting up the dirt path. It sat down and stared across with those pit-like eyes. Its fur was matted, and some of Jonah, who was currently stuck in the wheel well of a second bus attempting to brake, spattered near it. When the traffic stilled, it trotted over to her, leaning against her ankle in a reassuring manner.

That's when Suze realized she was the one screaming.

The last time the dog came to see her, Suze had been waiting for five years. Her thirtieth birthday was approaching, and she could feel the dog approaching as well. After Jonah's cremation (there hadn't been enough left of him to collect for a proper burial) she'd left the funeral with some of his ashes in a small blue urn, and immediately checked herself into a psychiatric ward. No one was really surprised by this; it was the third violent and deadly incident she had witnessed in as many decades. Most assumed that with the proper counseling and therapy, Suze would be fine.

The first time Suze told anyone about the dog was in a small grey room to a man in a white coat with wire-rimmed glasses that hung crooked on his nose. That was the first time her fear was dismissed as a "hallucination brought on as a psychiatric coping mechanism in the event of severe mental distress". By the fifth time, she knew it was better to keep her mouth shut.

They released her after six months, and she moved back into the small apartment she and Jonah had shared together. She waited there, but the dog never came. Not when her grandmother finally passed peacefully in her sleep. Not when Jonah's father, who had always made sure to keep checking on his dead son's girlfriend, died of cardiac arrest while hanging Christmas lights on the 12th of November. The dog was conspicuously absent, but Suze knew. She knew without a doubt it would be back.

Seven months before her birthday, she received the first letter in the mail. It was from a secret admirer. She had read it, carefully folded it up, and put it in one of her kitchen drawers relegated to those odd scraps of paper one finds around the house.

The second came two weeks later, and the third two days after that. They got more detailed, more insistent that Suze return the affection. They had no mailing address. It wasn't until one of the letters contained a picture of her leaving work that she called the police. They couldn't (wouldn't) do anything without a direct threat. The phone calls that followed, the missing trash bags, the flowers sent to her work—none of them were enough to garner the police's help. Like so many other victims, Suze was on her own.

Her apartment was broken into. She moved. It was broken into again. She felt a hollow space fill up the part of her chest where her heart was supposed to be. Daily terror had changed her, like waves beating upon the shore until it had smoothed her jagged edges and dulled her terror to a quiet expectation. She waited.

And now it was the eve of her thirtieth birthday. She had come home from work to her dark apartment. She always left the lights off out of habit now. This way, nobody—and a particular nobody—would know if she was inside.

All day long, something had been building. When she got home, she sat down on her couch, closed her eyes, and waited with a certainty that didn't betray her.

At half-past eight, something scratched at the door. It was the scratch of an animal that wanted to be let out or, in this particular case, in. It was insistent, pausing every few seconds before beginning up again. Suze didn't realize she was crying until she stood up and went to the door. She unlocked the three locks she'd had installed and opened the door a crack. A small shape slithered in from the dingy hall. A familiar face looked up at her, as solemn and expectant as she was.

She locked the door again and went back to the couch. The dog followed her, its black eyes never leaving her face. It panted, as if stressed.

She sat down, picked up her cell phone. It was low, practically dead. She dialed a number.

"911, What's your emergency?"

Her apartment was closest to the fire-escape stairs, where she now heard heavy footsteps ascending and then coming down the hallway.

"Hello? 911, What's your emergency?"

The dog stood up and took a few steps towards the door, its ears perked.

"I'm going to die tonight," Suze said finally.

"Ma'am? Is everything okay?"

Someone was standing outside her door. They were breathing heavily. She could hear them shuddering on the intake.

"Someone is going to break into my apartment and kill me," Suze said. Someone knocked.

"Please help me," Suze said. The knocking stopped for a moment, and then started again.

The dog came over and licked her palm. It looked at her and wagged its tail.

"Ma'am?"

She told the operator her address. The knocking on her door got louder, more insistent.

"Ma'am, someone is on their—" The phone died. Suze stared at it, sitting in the dark as the rhythmic pounding became erratic and enraged. Her heart pounded in time with it. She went into the kitchen and grabbed a knife from the carving block. The dog looked at her. She looked at the knife and the dog and then the knife again and knew that it wouldn't do any good.

She sat on the floor cross-legged, and the small dog crawled into her lap. Its matted fur was cold and stank of decay as she wrapped her arms around it. She held it tight. It had no heartbeat. Suze tried to stop crying, but she couldn't. Someone rammed their body against the door. It groaned and creaked.

She knew what was about to happen.

She hoped that it wouldn't hurt for too long.

She hoped she could be brave—and she was.

She only started screaming after the door splintered open.

HIBERNACULUM

THE CEILING SEETHED with snakes. Marcus could see them crawling over one another, their tails thrashing, a reptilian Gordian knot that extended throughout his entire studio apartment. They pressed through the drywall, peering down through the recessed lighting, tongues flickering with the lights. Their shapes and movements were as prominent as if the walls were tissue paper. He thought at first it was just a bad trip, but when he woke up and the mushrooms had worn off, he could still see them writhing.

He stared up at the ceiling as it moved. It reminded him of water; the way the drywall wavered was like surface ripples interrupting the calm surface of a lake. The ripples cascaded down the walls like a grotesque waterfall. He thought he could hear something moving under the floorboards.

"Fuck this," he said, and ran up the stairs and out of his private entrance. Shivering in his boxers, he pounded on his landlord's door. "Luke! Fuck man, get out here!"

Luke's wife, Rhiannon, opened the door and stared at him with a critical eye. Her young son peered around her leg. "What do you want? Where are your clothes?"

"The basement is fucking full of snakes," Marcus snapped at her. "I thought you might want to know. This is unsanitary."

"Snakes?" The young boy's head snapped up to peer at Marcus's sweaty face as his mother spoke. Her face paled, her mouth tightening. "What do you mean, it's full of snakes?" she said in a clipped tone.

"I mean, it's *full of fucking snakes*. I can see them everywhere. They're in the walls, in the ceiling. Pretty sure they're in the floor."

Rhiannon threw her head back and yelled into the house. "Luke, we need you!" She frowned at Marcus. "Do you mind watching your language around the kids?" she asked curtly. Marcus just stared at her incredulously.

Luke arrived at the front door, his t-shirt and beard still coated with toast crumbs. "Hey Marcus, what's up?"

"The basement is full of snakes!"

Luke fixed him with a confused stare, arching a bushy eyebrow. "Snakes?"

"Yes, snakes," Marcus snapped. "Hundreds of fucking snakes. I thought you would be more concerned about the house being infested with reptiles."

Luke and his wife exchanged glances, and she guided her son back inside. Luke raised his hands in a consoling manner.

"Sorry, dude, but we haven't seen any snakes."

"Can you at least come check the goddamn basement out? I pay good money to live there."

"Yeah, man, just give me a minute." Luke closed the door, and Marcus stood there, shifting from foot to foot. Luke opened the door after a minute, shoes on, and tossed Marcus a worn bathrobe.

"It's October," he explained, as Marcus shrugged into it. "You really shouldn't be going around in the cold dressed like that."

"I was more worried about the fucking snakes than I was about getting dressed," Marcus grumped.

"I heard you the first time."

As they came around the side of the house, Marcus hesitated. The door was open, and he hadn't turned on the stairwell light. The entryway reminded him of the throat of an underground monster, leading down into a dark and hungry stomach. It was only twelve steps down to his apartment, but he couldn't see the bottom. It made him uneasy.

Luke noticed his hesitation and took the lead. He entered first, walking down the gaping gullet into the belly of the beast. Marcus waited until the light flickered on, and then slowly descended, wrapping Luke's dressing gown tightly around himself.

He stepped down into his apartment. The walls were still moving, and he could see the shape of something very large slithering across the ceiling and into the bathroom.

"Dude, what the hell!?" Luke said.

"Right?! I mean—" Marcus started, but Luke just waved at the coffee table in front of the sagging couch. It was littered with weed nuggets, a filthy bong, and a half-smoked joint.

"We said no drugs in the house. We have *kids*, dude, and we share the same air. Clean this shit up." Luke glowered at him, hands shoved into his pockets. "Seriously, this is not cool."

Behind him, the wall shifted, sleek muscular shapes crawling over one another.

"Fine, I'll clean up the pot, but what about the fucking snakes?! Look at the walls!"

"Are you okay? I don't see any snakes. Where did you say they were?"

Marcus stared at him. Luke moved through the apartment, peering into corners, lifting up pieces of furniture and looking underneath them. The walls continued to squirm.

"I'm not seeing any snakes. Did you take something?" Luke eyed the scum-encrusted table.

"No," Marcus said, ignoring the memory of the capsules filled with "Godzilla Penis Envy" shrooms he'd swallowed down last night and chased with a beer. "Are you sure you don't see any snakes?"

"No man, not at all." One of the pot lights flickered as a long, lean body slithered across it from the inside. Luke didn't seem to notice. "I'm not saying there aren't snakes, but like, I don't see any. If you do see anymore, keep your phone handy and send me a picture, and I'll get someone in to deal with it."

"You aren't going to do that now?" Marcus asked, incredulous.

Luke shrugged. "I don't see any snakes, man, much less hundreds of them. I'm not going to pay out the nose to have animal control or an exterminator or whoever you call for snakes come in when there isn't a problem. If you want someone to come check up on it, you can pay for it."

"Cool, thanks." Marcus ripped off the robe and threw it at him.

"No problem," Luke said blithely, catching it and going up the stairs without another word.

Marcus sat on the couch and listened to the light murmuring of Luke and his wife through the ceiling. They were probably talking about how crazy their tenant was.

The floor moved underneath his feet, and he yanked them up. He didn't think he was still high, but he had a shift at the restaurant he worked at as a short-order cook, so maybe by the time he got back, the shrooms would have worn off and the snakes would be gone.

Eight hours of flinging burgers and being spattered with fry grease didn't change his mood. He snarled at the dish-boy, burnt the side of his hand on the flattop, and nearly made a waitress cry when she came back with a plate of food. His manager yelled at him and told him to go take an extra smoke break and lose the attitude.

Through it all, he didn't see a single snake.

When he arrived home, he steeled himself before inserting the key into his lock. It turned with a click, and he opened the door. He had left the light on, and as he headed inside, he noticed a mild, musky smell that grew with every step. By the time he'd transitioned onto the scuffed laminate flooring, his home lay out before him like a horror movie. The snakes seemed to have multiplied. They pressed hard against the inside of the walls, which bowed outwards with the sheer number of the reptilian invaders. It was unusually hot in the basement, which only amplified the smell. He ran to the windows, throwing them open and breathing in the cool October air. Then he noticed a subtle hissing. It wasn't the sound of tongues flicking in and out. It took him a moment before he realized it was the sound of many scales slipping over each other, rasping like sandpaper. His stomach churned.

The movement of the walls slowed as the cold air circulated. His hands shook as he pulled out his phone and dialed his friend Nate. He asked him to come over for a second. Nate lived with his parents down the road, and he was over in ten minutes, finding Marcus standing outside his door, trembling.

"Yo, what's wrong?"

Marcus just pointed down into his apartment. Nate shot him a strange look and noisily clomped down the stairs. Marcus waited to see if he started screaming, but it was quiet.

"Dude, are you coming or what? Also, it's fucking cold down here. I'm closing your windows."

Marcus re-entered the basement and had his confirmation. Nate was already lighting up, sprawled out on the couch. Nate couldn't see the snakes either, couldn't see the way they continued pushing into the room, or the way they writhed in what Marcus interpreted as eager anticipation. He took a deep breath. He must be losing his mind. Forcing a stiff smile, he sat next to Nate, took the joint from his fingers and deeply inhaled.

"What was it you wanted to show me?" Nate asked, but Marcus just shook his head and took another drag.

"Nevermind."

Nate spent an hour with him, nattering on about the latest TV series he was binging. Marcus stared at his feet, making affirmative noises at the correct time, unable to understand why Nate couldn't see what he saw.

After Nate left, Marcus fell into a fitful sleep, doing his best to imagine the sound of scales slipping over one another was the sound of waves breaking against a shore. He dreamt of an ocean of snakes crashing against the shore, slithering up the sand towards him. He fled, feet sinking in dunes that turned to sidewinders. He woke up drenched in sweat that beaded up on his skin with an acrid smell that reminded him of venom.

He called animal control as soon as they were open. The woman who answered was a little confused, but quickly passed the phone to a man who had a little more knowledge of reptiles.

"And you say there are how many snakes?"

Marcus looked around at the seething walls and ceiling of his apartment. "Hundreds."

"What size are they?"

The walls teemed. Marcus tried to gauge. He could see huge ones, ones like pythons, and small ones barely the size of his pinkie finger, all of them swarming over each other in a manner that made it hard to tell where one ended and another began.

"All sizes," he replied. The man whistled.

"It is almost winter—usually by now most snakes have entered their hibernaculum—the place where they wait out the winter. They do it in groups, yeah, but hundreds is beyond what I would expect, especially considering you're in the suburbs. What was your address again?"

Marcus told him.

"Yeah, that doesn't make a lot of sense. You might have a few garter snakes in that area, maybe, and just maybe, a lost rat snake or two, but hundreds infesting a single house wouldn't happen. What did you say they looked like? Like, what is their colouration?"

"I don't know, I can't see them."

There was a pause at the other end.

"You can't see them?" the man spoke slowly.

"I know they are there," Marcus said, panic entering his voice. His tongue tripped over his teeth. "I *know* they are there."

"Look, buddy," the guy on the phone said. "I'm not sure I can help you. Maybe you should call someone else. Like your doctor."

The line went dead.

Marcus gulped, his eyes fixed on the walls. They pushed outwards ominously, throbbing, like the apartment itself were alive. He had the horrible feeling he had already been swallowed by a gargantuan serpent, and he was watching it breathe from the inside. In and out, in and out, that horribly slithering now joined with the sound of a thousand forked tongues hissing in unison. Heat rolled through the basement, alternating waves of dry and humid warmth that had sweat pouring down Marcus's skin. It dripped off of him onto a floor that roiled like a boat with the force of the imminent invasion.

The air thickened with that musty odor, forcing itself down his throat and nostrils. He began to cough, the musk choking him. When he tried to throw open the window again, the latch stuck. He scrabbled at it and saw the first flakes of the first snow drift down into the window well. He took a few steps back and turned to flee.

He was too late. The walls burst open, the paint peeling away like diseased skin. The ceiling disintegrated. Snakes fountained up through the floor. A torrent poured from the ceiling. Marcus yelped, throwing himself back onto his bed. They followed him, and a waterfall continued to crash down onto him. The snakes moved over him, a warm and wiggling weight that pinned him in place. The feel of their scales against his bare skin was revolting, and the tongue of one reached out to vibrate against his cheek, smelling him, caressing him. They wound across the floors, flowing together like a horrible river, drawn to him as if they were moths and he were a flame.

He tried to scream, but a large, thick shape slithered across his head, muffling his cries. He tried to reach up to yank it away, pulling the snakes off of him and flinging them wildly. Multiple sets of fangs sank into him with bolts of white-hot agony. All he could do was moan, but as soon as his lips parted, the snakes moved towards his face.

He choked as one began to slither down his throat.

The following week, when Marcus missed rent and wouldn't respond to any calls or texts or polite knocks, Luke took his key and opened the door. One whiff of the stale, musky air was all it took before he slammed the door shut, his shirt covering his mouth as he gagged.

When the authorities came—the ambulance, the fire department, and the police all running lights—it drew a large crowd of neighbors, who chatted amongst themselves. Luke also called animal control. "It stinks like the reptile house in the zoo," he said to the lady on the other end of the phone. "He told me that there were hundreds of snakes, but I never saw any."

When they entered, it was a scene from a nightmare. The basement was filled with snakeskin—small and large, entire sheathes of animals that had been there and gone, serpentine ghosts that draped across furniture and piles of musty clothes. On the bed lay what remained of Marcus—a hollow bag of what was once a human being, mouth stretched unnaturally wide.

He was deflated, his skin like parchment. He was so light as to be almost air—like a balloon, his skin dried and cracked. His eyelids were closed, and when a firefighter held a flashlight against his cheek, he lit up like a paper lamp, and the poor man ran outside to empty the contents of his stomach.

They never found a single snake—not a living one, not a body, not a bone. They never found any droppings either, or eggs, or even slither marks in the buildup of dust. The walls and ceiling were smooth, the paint unmarred. All they found was the hundreds of shed snakeskins littering the basement. When they finally cut what was left of Marcus open in an attempt to find out what exactly happened to him, they found that his organs, his muscles, and his veins were all gone. All that remained was his own discarded skin, and in the cavity where his stomach should have been, was the largest snakeskin of them all.

THE PANTRY

THE STATE OF things in the nursing home was unpleasant. The facility was considered the "budget" option for the elderly; the bulk of our residents were people with no friends or family, meager estates, and nowhere else to go. Our threadbare carpets, dim lighting, and scuffed walls were the last shabby stop for many. Every few days we would wheel someone on a squeaking gurney out the back door, silent and still and shrouded in a familiar black bag.

During the night shift, we operated with a skeleton staff. Just a few exhausted CNAs and PSWs struggling to get the never-ending list of night work done and failing horribly, lorded over by the solo night nurse on duty. Nurse Horace, called Horrid behind her back, would endlessly and bitterly complain about our work ethic as she ordered us around loudly from the small front office she had claimed as her own. She spent most of her nights there, shuffling around the stacks of papers on her desk and glaring at us nastily. It was a miserable place to work.

My last night on the job began the same as any other. I clocked in, made the rounds and checked on the residents, dealt with some crisis, tried to catch up on paperwork, dealt with another crisis, called the paramedics, called the morgue, dealt with yet another crisis. It was an endless carousel

of drudgery and depression. As always, Nurse Horrid just sat there, her beady eyes watching us from the rolling desk chair that served as her dark throne. She was supposed to be doing much more than that in terms of physical workload, but no matter how many complaints directed towards upper management, they were always ignored. Nurse Horrid, much to our dismay, wasn't doing anything and wasn't going anywhere.

There was only one thing Nurse Horrid insisted on doing both herself and by herself every night: the medication rounds. She would break up her shift with a stint in the pharmaceutical closet, stuffing herself into the cramped space and overflowing out into the hallway. She wasn't heavy, she was *engorged*. The sort of swelling we'd see in patients with severe lymphedema. She would carefully count out the dosages with her thick fingers, and after she had double and triple-checked, she would lumber out with the tray precariously perched on her puffy forearms, skin pulled taut around her distended and lumpy hands. She would make the deliveries, walking through the building in her awkward and ungainly way, going into every room to administer the prescriptions, shots, and assorted vitamins meant to stave off the vultures circling our residents. She would take her sweet time completing this task, and we would all do our best to stay out of her way, ducking into the ancient staff room-slash-kitchen and taking a much-needed break when she wasn't watching.

That night, Nurse Horrid went to make her rounds. She left her cellphone sitting on her desk as she always did, but to our surprise we heard it ring for the first time ever. It rang and it rang and it rang, the shrill default ringtone echoing through the lower level of the building. It was at full-volume, and we worried it would wake the residents. The PSWs debated among ourselves what we should do; whether we should answer it, ignore it, or turn the volume down. It was decided the best course of action was to bring the troublesome thing to her so she couldn't accuse us of tampering with or trying to steal the damn thing. I lost several frantic rounds of rock, paper, scissors and had to grab the still-ringing phone from her desk. While my grateful co-workers remained behind and cowered, I went in search of Nurse Horrid.

It took me a while to find her. The door of a Mr. Lester Adamik was cracked open, a strange noise coming from within. Mr. Adamik had been rapidly declining over the last few days, and I initially thought Nurse Horrid had been helping him through some sort of medical episode.

"Ma'am," I said timidly as I entered the room. "Your phone wouldn't stop ringing. I brought it to you—there might be an emergency."

She was bent over the prone Mr. Adamik, her squat bulk momentarily blocking him from view. I heard him gasping, and when the phone rang again, she turned to me with an audible swallow as she wiped her mouth with the back of a fleshy hand. Her beady eyes focused on me, and a chill ran down my spine.

Something was different. There was a malevolence about her that hadn't been there before, a strange aura that warned some ancient part of my brain that this was a predator and a threat and that I *should not move*. I froze, barely breathing, the ringing phone still clutched in my hand.

Her hateful eyes narrowed. The distorted light from the small and filthy window next to the bed fell across her face in such a way that it made it seem like there were a dozen of them. They blinked in unison, and then there were only two again.

"Get out," she hissed, two dripping fangs filling her mouth and grotesquely distorting her words. It was then that the shadow on the opposite wall of the window began to move, and I realized with a dawning horror that the thing projected across the wall was not the shadow of the woman in front of me.

It was the shadow of a giant spider attached to Nurse Horrid's swollen feet, a thing with a massive bloated abdomen and eight huge and hairy legs that stretched grotesquely across the wall. As she moved away from the bed, a desiccated Mr. Adamik now rattled with every breath. I could see no visible puncture marks on him, but even if I had they wouldn't be out of place on the papery skin of the residents; skin that was already torn and blooming with bruises like a garden of death was the perfect camouflage for a well-hidden feeding. There was a final rattle, and the room fell silent except for the ringing of the phone. Mr. Adamik was dead.

My mind rushed through the names of the recently deceased; how many was she responsible for? How many had she drained? *What was she?*

I fumbled with the phone and handed it to her. She smiled, and the legs across the wall began to skitter towards me with a dark intent. I fled then, turning my back and running through the labyrinthine halls, my eyes watering and my heart in my throat, and hid for the rest of the night. The next morning, I handed in my immediate resignation, scrawled on the back of a crumbled invoice I had plucked from the kitchen garbage.

I do not drive by the nursing home anymore, nor do I speak to my old coworkers. I've put that place entirely behind me, though that does not stop the nightmares. I still dream of a giant torpid spider who does not need a web, growing fat and hateful while her meals, alone and already reeking of death, are delivered to her in hospital beds.

She waits for me there, too, hoping I return. I know more certainly than anything else in my life that if I were ever to step foot into Nurse Horrid's pantry again, I would never step back out.

THE NIGHT DENTIST

It was 1:02 a.m., and Melissa Abernathy was in agony. She gave up on her attempts to sleep. Her tossing and turning sent bolts of lightning shooting through her jaw, suggesting it was time for immediate medical care. She rolled over to grab her phone from the tilted bedside table that was only held together by duct tape and dreams, and opened her web browser. She haltingly typed in the name of her town and "emergency dentist". The local small-town urgent care was closed now, and she didn't want to travel to the hospital in the next big city over. Not only was she afraid she couldn't drive that far in this state, but the cost of an emergency hospital visit would be prohibitive. She was better off finding a still-prohibitive-but-probably-less-expensive-actual dentist.

She hoped to find an early morning appointment somewhere, anywhere, but every online scheduling form for any dentist nearby told her there weren't appointments available the next day and that a receptionist would be in touch with her...eventually.

In despair, she clicked through to the second page of listings, and right at the bottom of the page was an entry just called "The Night Dentist". It had no photos, no reviews, and no real information. It looked to have opened recently. She tapped through to a sleek-looking website, as clean

and sterile as any dental instrument. Their information page told her they were a practice dedicated to night-shift workers or those in need of emergency dental care. There wasn't a portal through which she could book an appointment, but there was a phone number. She felt a small twinge of hope—perhaps she would not have to wait until morning after all.

When she dialed the number, she was surprised to hear only a series of crackles and pops within a blanket of white static. The phone must not have been connected yet. Her heart sank into her stomach. Even that brought a twinge of pain to her jaw, and she winced. She thought of ending the call when she heard a faint click before a robotic voice began to speak.

"Thank you for calling The Night Dentist. You have reached our automated menu. The Night Dentist is currently with a client and unavailable to answer the phone. If you are looking for emergency dental work, please press one. If you are a registered patient with us, please press two." She pressed one so fast her finger slid along her phone screen. There was a strange grinding noise, and the phone turned to static again. She waited for a full minute and drifted back off to sleep before the metallic voice, now with a distinct echo behind it, startled her awake.

"The Night Dentist will see you now," it said, and then the line went dead.

She stared at it for a moment before redialing. The automated message did not return—there was the same strange grinding noise, and then the voice returned.

"The Night Dentist will see you now," it intoned. "Our address is Unit 221b...." it rattled off basic directions before the line went dead again. Her jaw throbbed, her ear ached, and she was reminded that despite the strangeness of it all she could not afford to wait. She threw on a pair of loose linen pants and grabbed her keys from where they lay on the chipped laminate kitchen countertop. Within minutes she was out of her apartment, the door slamming shut behind her.

She quickly came to the outer limits of the town and turned onto a rural route indicated only by a number. She followed her GPS as it instructed her in its monotone voice to zigzag her way through the unfamiliar back roads. Every bump and rattle along the gravel was like a dagger in her skull.

It seemed like an eternity had passed when her phone finally announced her destination was on the left. She put her foot on the brake, coming to a rough halt in front of what was clearly a construction zone in the middle of absolutely nowhere.

Beside her, freshly laid pavement attached what was still the bare bones of a plaza to the gravel road. Only one side of the three-sided plaza was complete; four storefronts lined up, all of them empty, their black windows like cavernous, empty mouths. A second side was half complete, with two stores fully built and two of them still missing windows and covered in scaffolding. The third side was literally bare bones, with only the metal structural beams in place. Melissa thought it was odd that it had been constructed in such a manner—it reminded her of a paintbrush swept across a canvas, the colour and shape fading the further it went on.

There were no parking lot lights, only hastily erected work lights everywhere pointed in random directions, sending thick beams of light cutting through the encroaching dark. It was in the half-constructed block that she saw more lights, pouring out the front windows of the left of the building. A blue neon sign above the door simply said "The Night Dentist" in a blocky font.

She pulled in and parked—the lines demarcating the parking spots had not been painted yet, so she half-guessed at where she was supposed to stop. She sat for a moment in the front seat, staring at the door to the dentist's office. Fear sloshed in her belly, souring it like a bottle of bad wine. A cold sweat broke out on her back. She closed her eyes and took a deep breath. Eyes still closed, she grabbed for her purse and exited her car, taking a few hesitant steps towards the front door.

Out here past the town limits, the air was strangely cool. She could hear the sound of crickets in the neighboring fields, the call of a night bird. A light breeze ruffled the back of her hair, encouraging her to move up to the lumpy sidewalk just outside of the office.

Peering into the window showed her an empty waiting room. When she gave the door an experimental tug, it opened so smoothly and weightlessly that she lost her balance and fell back a step. The unexpected movement rattled her jaw, eliciting a soft moan and reminding her how badly she needed to go in. Mustering up her courage, she entered the building.

The inside of the office was decorated in an incredibly modern style. Black imitation leather chairs not unlike the ones that stood around her dining room table lined the walls. They were new—she could smell their fresh-from-the-plastic scent from here, and not a single one had an indentation or crease from use on its smooth surface. The floor was polished white tile, an imitation marble shot through with black veins. The walls were a sterile white, broken up by a dozen black-framed pictures of what appeared to be a repeating modernist pattern of white blotches on a black velvety background. Gentle elevator music played, but in the background she could hear a low thrum that reminded her of an electrical transformer. The overall atmosphere of the place left her with a mild sense of disorientation.

She approached the desk, noting the sleek black monitor atop it. The screen was dark. A small hallway, painted black with black doors, led off to the left of the desk.

"Hello," she said, talking around her sore tooth. "Is anyone here? I need some help."

There was no answer.

Melissa glanced back outside at her car, wondering if this had all been an enormous mistake. Maybe she was currently trespassing, maybe police were coming to arrest her now. Exhaustion and pain weighed down her limbs. She was three seconds from bursting into tears.

"Hello," said a mild voice behind her. She turned, startled, to see a man standing behind the desk, dressed in scrubs underneath a white coat. His light brown hair was cropped close to his skull, and round wire-rimmed glasses sat on a button nose situated in what was an entirely unremarkable face. Bland, she thought, as she took in his medium height, medium physique, and brown eyes. There was nothing distinguishing about him whatsoever. She could have passed him on the street a hundred times and never realized it.

"How can I help you?" he asked, oblivious to her train of thought.

She gestured to her mouth. "I need help," she said, her tongue like cotton in her mouth. "I have this horrible toothache."

He assessed her quietly, taking in her tear-stained face and rumpled clothing. He reached out a neatly manicured hand towards her face, as if to touch her swollen jaw, and then drew it back quickly.

"Follow me," he said in a kind voice. "It's a good thing it's a quiet night—you're my first patient of the evening." He turned briskly and set off down the small hall.

She followed him hesitantly. The hallway was long, extending further back than it looked from the outside. The black doors that lined the hallway were all closed. There were an awful lot of them. There was no artwork here—just smooth walls that seemed abnormally tall. The whole place reminded her of a carnival funhouse.

Ahead of her, the dentist's brown dress shoes clacked against the tile flooring. With each step she took, the conflagration of torment in her mouth was stoked higher and higher. The pain grew and grew until she was practically stumbling, sweat pouring down her forehead into her eyes and stinging them. The dentist cast a sympathetic look backwards over his shoulder.

"Don't you worry, we'll get you sorted out in no time, Miss Abernathy," he said as they came to the door at the very end of the hallway. He took a key out of the breast pocket of his dull blue scrubs to open it. The key was very large and looked like an antique, with an elaborate filigree handle in tarnished silver. It seemed drastically out of place in the modern office, and she wondered what exactly the key was for.

To her surprise, he slid it neatly into the lock of the door they were standing in front of, and he turned it with a quick wrench. He opened the door and stood just inside, holding it open for her. "Let's get you into the chair and we'll see what can be done."

She walked timidly over to the pristine white chair in the centre of the room. The white sink next to it was also immaculate and gleamed with an almost otherworldly brightness. A tray on wheels held a black velvet cloth, upon which multiple dental instruments sat waiting. She crawled into the chair, turning around. It felt as if her jaw was about to explode. Tears streamed down her face, and her nose started to run.

The dentist followed her, positioning the bright light overtop of them so that it shone directly into Melissa's eyes. She squinted and blinked, looking away and around the room.

Like the hallway, the walls in here were painted solid pitch black, as was the ceiling, though it was studded with pot lights. She was dizzy for a moment, stuck within a strangely cuboid void, untethered from the rest of the world.

Despite this odd choice of paint colour, the room was fairly well lit. The walls were also otherwise unornamented. Black cabinets lined one wall with white pulls, giving off the strange optical illusion that the hardware was floating. However, it was the left wall that really drew her attention as the dentist sat on a rolling stool and scooted towards her.

It was a massive aquarium. It was unlit, and it stretched from floor to ceiling and wall to wall. The glass was very thick and very clean, without so much as a smudge or a fingerprint marring its polished surface. She could see darker shadows within its depths—what she thought might be a large piece of decorative driftwood, the long tendrils of an underwater plant that gently swayed within the unseen current. Something large—a fish, perhaps—darted in and out of the darkest areas of the tank, always managing to stay just out of sight.

The dentist followed her gaze. "Beautiful, isn't it? Aquariums are my hobby. I insisted on having one built into the office."

Melissa nodded. She'd never seen anything like it, and she kept her eye on it as she settled back downwards. She closed her eyes as he hovered over top of her, gently placing his fingers on her cheek.

"Open your mouth, please."

She obliged, giving an involuntary groan as he tilted her chin up, looking inside of her mouth, his brow furrowing. His other hand moved to the silver instruments next to him, selecting one by touch alone. He poked it into her mouth. Melissa squeezed her eyes shut tightly, trying not to think about his probing fingers.

"This...does not look good," he said slowly. "I'm going to need to numb the area to do a proper examination. I'll use a topical gel at first, and then after a minute, I'll have to use a needle to finish numbing it."

Melissa felt like she was going to throw up. The dentist squeezed out the contents of a small tube onto his index finger and swiped it along the inside of her mouth around her swollen gum. It began to work almost immediately, offering her a small reprieve.

The dentist stood up and crossed to the cabinets. She couldn't see what he was doing, but he rummaged around for a minute before he returned, a long silver needle held in his hand. Melissa audibly gulped.

"You won't feel this, not really," he said with a small smile. Before she could respond, he quickly jabbed it into her mouth. There was a small pinprick feeling, and the salt of blood hitting her tongue. There was a long moment as he depressed the plunger, and then numbness completely overtook her mouth. She moaned with relief as the remainder of the pain vanished in a rush of cold. The dentist's blue-gloved hands gently opened her jaw wider and peered into it, his hands switching out multiple instruments as he poked and prodded at the source of the pain.

"This tooth is entirely rotted through," the night dentist murmured to her. "You must have been in agony."

Melissa tried to nod, her eyes watering. With the numbing having taken effect, she found a tsunami of fear waiting for her. It crashed into her almost physically, her heart pounding. Her limbs began to tingle as her muscles tensed. She felt sick to her stomach.

The dentist noticed the change in her, and he gave her a sympathetic look. "Not a fan of dentists, eh?"

She shook her head. Her throat clenched, and she began to shake. The dentist went to the cupboard again and pulled out a small weighted lap blanket, throwing it over her legs. It helped, and in a moment she stopped trembling.

"I wish I had better news for you," he said with a grimace, "But I'm going to have to remove the tooth. It needs to come out immediately."

"I don't think I can sit still for that," Melissa gulped, her tongue fuzzy and her words blurry around the edges. "Is there any other way?" She wondered if this was just a night terror, a horrible dream caused by the agony of an abscessed tooth, if she was still back in her sweltering apartment on her uncomfortable twin bed. She hoped she was.

"It will be the quickest way," the dentist said sympathetically. "I need to get to the source of the infection and clean it out, and it's so pitted with cavities that I would need to reconstruct it entirely. Best to pull it out now, clean you up, and then do a followup appointment." He hesitated for a moment. "If you are concerned about moving during the extraction, there are some restraints attached to your chair. Nothing too serious, mind you. They are just heavy-duty Velcro. We have had several patients in the past who reacted poorly to anesthesia and became violent. If you want, we can tie your wrists down if you feel you might hinder the extraction.

"It has to come out? Right now?" Melissa's chest heaved. Her lungs filled with liquid panic that threatened to drown her.

"The infection is already quite advanced," the dentist said. "Any further, and I would recommend an emergency hospital visit and probably an extended stay. Untreated tooth decay can lead to sepsis or even heart attacks. Back before the advent of modern dentistry, a lot of deaths could be attributed to poor tooth health. If you would prefer, I can call an ambulance, but at this point the sooner it comes out, the better. Would you like to use the restraints?"

She could barely breathe, much less speak. She nodded, swallowing down the bile burning her throat.

"You can do the first hand," the dentist offered gently. She inserted her left hand, crossing the strap over and pulling it tight. He came over and did her right hand for her. His skin was soft and cool to the touch where his fingertips grazed the inside of her wrist. "You just tell me if you want them off, and they'll come off." Melissa nodded mutely. "I have to go get a few instruments from the other exam room. I'll be right back."

He was gone only for a moment, but during those seconds, the shadow in the tank revealed itself, darting out of the shadows with a powerful swish of its tail.

It was a largemouth bass—bigger than any specimen she had ever seen, easily the size of a small child. Melissa grew up fishing with her dad, and she had caught a lot of whoppers, but she had never seen one this size. It reminded her of something she had seen in a natural history museum, an ancient and primeval creature. It made the hairs rise on her arms then and now.

It moved closer, silvery-green scales shimmering in the light. It swam back and forth along the length of the wall, moving closer and closer to her. It stopped as close as it could to her, so close that its nose was practically bumping up against the glass. The behavior triggered some instinctual fear in Melissa and she recoiled, pressing herself into the chair until the restraints pulled tightly at her wrists.

The fish's lips began to open, but horizontally instead of vertically. With a growing sense of horror, she realized the fish had teeth, a full set of adult *human* teeth, white and practically glowing underneath the light of the lamp. It was as if a set of dentures had been shoved within its fleshy mouth.

"Hello," the fish said, bubbles exploding outwards and rising to the top of the tank. Despite the separation by what had to be hundreds of gallons of water and thick glass, the words were only slightly muffled. She could see a long tongue within its mouth, also humanoid. "Welcome to the Night Dentist. I understand you're doing an extraction this evening?"

Melissa screamed.

The dentist ran back in, holding a tray of sterilized instruments. "Ms. Abernathy, is everything alright?"

"The fish, the fish spoke," she screeched. "It has teeth! Teeth!" She bucked against the arm restraints, a flailing leg nearly kicking the tray out of the dentist's hand. The dentist looked over at the tank and at the grinning face that floated there.

"There is no need to get hysterical," the dentist said in a patient tone. "This is my associate. I can assure you, he means you no harm. He observes my procedures. He is quite professional. I'm going to have to ask you to stop screaming."

Melisa didn't stop. The night dentist spoke again, more sternly this time.

"The numbing will wear off quicker than you think. We need to do the procedure immediately, or we will be forced to either start over or have you leave the premises."

The fish nodded, its face still stretched wide in a terrible grin.

"Would you prefer it if I called an ambulance?" the dentist asked with a bit of scorn. Melissa shook her head and clamped her lips shut as her final scream petered out. She could not afford an ambulance, much less what they would charge for a stay. She already had no idea how she was going to pay for this visit. The two fears warred for a moment inside of her, but her frugality won out.

"That's better," the fish said smugly, satisfied. "Now we can proceed with the extraction." It clacked its teeth together in an anticipatory manner. Melissa watched with wide eyes.

The dentist placed the new tray of instruments down on the rotating desk and sat back down.

"I need you to open your mouth," he said to Melissa. Melissa shook her head vehemently, glancing back at the aquarium and its nightmarish denizen. The dentist became visibly agitated.

"Ms. Abernathy," he sighed in irritation. "We don't have time for this. Every second we delay is a second the infection is closer to infecting your bloodstream. Now, either open your mouth, or get out of my office."

The fish shook its head disapprovingly at her. The strangeness of the experience thus far, the remaining pain, the fear of everything finally broke Melissa. Silently, she did as she was told, she opened her numbed mouth.

The dentist put on a headlight and flicked it on, then adjusted the overhead light so that he could see better.

"There we go," he said. His hand hovered over his instruments. Dread squeezed Melissa's heart. "Thank you for your cooperation."

He held up what appeared to be a large set of pliers, showing them to both Melissa and the fish.

"Excellent choice," the fish said with an approving nod. "Different from your usual, but impeccable thinking on your part."

"Why, thank you," the dentist replied. "I appreciate the kind words."

He loomed over Melissa, and without another word, he roughly grabbed her cheeks in his hand, forcing her mouth open wider. The smell of the latex gloves filled her nose, and then she felt the pliers compress her tongue as they made their way to the back of her jaw.

She tried not to whimper, focusing her eyes on a spot on the dentist's forehead. There was a crinkle there as he stared at her with intense concentration, jamming the fingers of his other hand into her mouth. Her brain tried to tell her he was about to shove his hand all the way into her mouth, jamming his overeager fingers into her throat, down, down, down into her chest cavity so he could squeeze her heart into a messy pulp. No matter how hard she tried to silence that thought, it was unsuccessful.

She felt the pliers latch onto her bad tooth and begin to pull.

White light flashed before her eyes, striking again and again as he tugged. She could hear her tooth beginning to crack under the strain. Despite the numbing, hot fire traced up her jaw, and she moaned through her full mouth.

"Now, now. Ms. Abernathy, was it?" the fish said. "None of that. Let the man concentrate."

Sweat beaded on the dentist's forehead as he wiggled the tooth roughly back and forth in her infected gum. The corners of his lips twitched up into a smile that broke his stoic face. He smiled and smiled, his mouth becoming too wide, mirroring the smile of the fish in the tank. She realized just how white his teeth were, how they seemed to fluoresce under the light. A long, moist tongue peeked out of the corner of his mouth, wriggling around like a thick pink worm.

Melissa opened and closed her hands as she struggled against the pain. The dentist leaned down, one bony elbow pinning her shoulder to contain her.

"You need to pull harder," the fish urged. The dentist grinned back at him maniacally, his eyes so bright they were practically fevered. He leveraged a foot up onto the chair and braced himself against it. The pressure in her mouth intensified, and Melissa's eyes rolled back in her head, her legs spasming in her panic.

"HARDER!" the fish screamed, and the dentist threw all his weight backwards with a triumphant yell.

The tooth came out.

The dentist crashed back onto the ground, his glasses askew, still grinning that terrible grin. Sweat glistened on his skin, and with triumph he held up the pair of forceps. Clutched between the pliers was a rotted tooth dripping a stinking mixture of blood and pus onto the floor next to him.

"Bravo!" the fish cried. "Bravo!"

In the chair, Melissa started to weep.

"You did superbly," the dentist said, not even bothering to look at her. "If you'll excuse me, I need a moment to compose myself." He stood up slowly and straightened his medical jacket and readjusted his scrubs. He dropped the rotted tooth into his hand and threw the pliers down with a clatter onto the other instruments. "I'll dispose of this while I'm at it." He held his palm up to his face, peering at the tooth closely. "Magnificent. A perfect extraction." He left the room without another word, ignoring the crying Melissa still strapped to the table.

The fish swam back and forth, doing several loop-de-loops. He stopped after a few seconds to peer down at Melissa.

"That wasn't so bad now, was it?"

Melissa whimpered again, squeezing her eyes shut and trying to ignore it.

"I must say though," it said, "you were a bit of a drama queen about the whole thing."

Melissa let out a long, shuddering breath.

"It's over now," she said, more to herself than anyone else. "It's over, no?"

"Oh, we've barely begun," the fish said jauntily. "Did you really think that he would stop at just taking the one?"

Its words took a moment to penetrate the fog of pain and fear clouding her brain. She burst upright, struggling against the restraints. They held fast. She kicked her legs, the tray of instruments clattering to the floor.

"Now, now, that's no way to behave," the fish chided. "We're all adults here."

A scream bubbled up through Melissa's chest and ripped through her throat. Blood-flecked spittle blew out from between her lips as she gasped with the exertion. She could taste infection on her tongue.

"Stop making such a big fuss. Stop it! Stop it! You're the one who called for a dentist," the fish said, darting back and forth. "Cut it out!"

She slammed her back down against the chair, propping her feet underneath her and arching her back and her arms. Her shoulders screamed in agony, but she felt one of the restraints begin to loosen.

"You are hardly being a model patient," the fish snarled. "Kindly compose yourself."

She did it again and again and again. It didn't take long before she could painfully squeeze and slip her left hand out of the Velcro binding. She rolled onto her side, her fingers scrabbling at the remaining restraint until she released herself. She fell off the chair, her knee banging painfully against the tiled floor. The freezing was wearing off. Her mouth began to throb again. She staggered upright, gripping the chair for balance.

"You won't get too far!" the fish called as it snapped its human teeth over and over again.. It slammed itself against the aquarium glass as if it meant to break it. "The extraction isn't over!"

Melissa ran to the door, fumbling with the lever handle. It was open, and she pushed through back into the hallway. The dentist was nowhere to be seen. She careened through the hallway and down into the reception area, stumbling until she tripped, falling behind the desk.

The empty desk. From this angle, she could see there was nothing on it. Not only was the computer screen dark, it wasn't even plugged in. When she touched it, she realized it was a hollow plastic model. There wasn't so much as a Post-It or a stapler. The binders on the shelves were very clearly empty, and there wasn't a card reader or cashbox.

As she looked around the room with eyes fairly unclouded by pain, she noticed that this was not a dentist's office, not truly; it was the shell of what was *supposed* to be a dentist's office, unfinished and rushed. It was a poor man's movie set, just the basics with no dressing, no substance. As she dashed to the front door, the pictures on the walls caught her attention. She'd been so blinded by pain earlier and thought they were abstract pieces, but now that she paused to examine one, her brain couldn't comprehend what she saw.

The pictures were of teeth. Full sets, all laid out and photographed. In each picture, there was one clearly rotten tooth. The rest of them looked relatively fine, though they were spattered and stained with what must have been blood. Their roots were all cracked in what must have been acts of incredible violence. She clapped her hand to her mouth, realizing the agony that these pictures represented. All those doors in the hallway... each one of them an exam room and a potential chamber of horrors. And Melissa had been so close to having her own teeth put on display on the waiting room wall.

Footsteps hurried down the hall, prompting her into motion again, throwing herself through the exit. She exploded out into the night air, which was so cold she could see her breath. The work lights were off, their bulbs smashed and their metal bodies crushed and distorted. The sky overhead was pitch black. There were no stars, and the crickets had stopped chirping.

She rushed to her car, throwing open the door and swinging herself inside with a smooth movement. She fumbled with her keys for just a second before jamming them in the ignition. The engine turned over, and she slammed on the gas.

As she peeled out of the parking lot and back into a world where there were stars and summer heat, blood oozed from the corner of her mouth. She looked back only once and saw for the last time the silhouette of the Night Dentist in the front window of his office, his glasses gleaming, face invisible in the gloom.

He lifted his hand, and waved.

COMMUNION

Historian's Note: The following excerpts are from the journal of the nun Hermana Floriana de Olmedo as found within the library of St. Joséph's Convent in Ávila, Spain. De Olmedo's journal is the only surviving account of the 1568 massacre in the town of Deia by the Spanish Inquisition.

14 July, Year of our Lord 1568

Today was the Sabbath, and the spirit of God was with us so strongly during Mass that I grow weak at the memory of it. When my mother entered the church, she was consumed by holy fire as soon as she crossed the threshold, and she fell to the ground in convulsions. I personally do not know the exquisite agony of St. Anthony's fire, but I understand the way it traces through the body as it burns away the original sin. My father went to go aid her, but his hands are so swollen that it hurt for him to prop her up. He called Alonso and me over, and we held Mamá as she spasmed and screamed.

Around us, the other parishioners lingered, smiles on their lips as they watched her be rewarded for her piety; for Mamá to feel God's touch as soon as she walked into the church was a blessing upon our family. Papá waved to them, the blackness of his flaking fingers stark in the light from all the candles that Father Benito had lit in preparation for today's services. Our flickering shadows danced along the walls like hosts of angels, wings stretching up to the rafters in worship.

My head began to pound as God fully entered the Church—it is hard for me to behold Him in all His glory. Father Benito was like a prophet today. His voice kept trailing off during his sermon, his eyes becoming distant and unfocused as he quoted the gospels to us. When he was so overcome by Grace that the words stopped coming, we continued the chants and the calls without him. Old Maria was so eager in her devotion that she vomited several times and lay curled on the ground of the church, her eyes rolling back in her head as she communed with the Holy Spirit.

Just when I felt I might faint, it was time for communion, which always strengthens me. As we stood shaking and filed up to the altar to receive Christ's blood and flesh, I saw His spirit in the form of small black dots that danced before my eyes. As the other worshippers took the rye communion into their palms and placed it between their teeth, letting the Holy Spirit melt upon their tongues. I was so overcome that I fell prostrate to the ground, prayers pouring forth between my lips like water from a well. Father Benito knelt beside me and pressed the bread lovingly between my lips. It turned to flesh, filling my mouth with blood. Behind me, my younger brother Alonso wept.

We stayed there on holy ground until the candles guttered out and the tide of ecstasy had retreated. I am back in my own bed now, next to a snoring Alonso. I can hear Mamá weeping in her bed, the thrashing of Papá's limbs as he violently prays, trying to find solace in the temporary absence of God.

16 July, Year of our Lord 1568
Old Maria has gone to be with God. Mamá has not yet recovered from the Sabbath, and one of Father's hands has burst open, gangrenous sin seeping out of it in the form of pus. His eyes are fevered. The farm work

is going undone. Every night, we stagger to the church to kneel and pray before the altar.

18 July, Year of our Lord 1568

I have been considering traveling to a convent and taking my Holy Orders in service to the Lord. There is a nun I have heard mention of; Teresa of Ávila, who is apparently subject to the same ecstasies as we are. She has founded the Convento de San José. How wonderful it would be to meet her! However, I am afraid to leave this town, where every scrap of land and every household has been transitioned to holy ground. Here, people wander down the street in sacred hazes, their eyes fixed unseeing on the face of God as they converse with Him. Even now, I can feel Him writhing underneath my skin, tracing His fingers behind my eyes. I can't help but shiver endlessly at the feel of His touch, my stomach churning with warmth and excitement. We are God's chosen people—how could anywhere else ever compare to this?

19 July, Year of our Lord 1568

Today, the holy spasms finally blessed me. Father Benito was with me when I came back into myself. He asked me what I had seen. I told him I didn't remember. He seemed disappointed, but he then invited me to the church. He asked that I aid in the creation of Holy Communion and make the wafers that would become the body of Christ during the ritual of transubstantiation. I have assisted Father Benito in many ways before—it was he who first noticed my aptitude with the written word— but not like this.

To say it was an honour was an understatement. I ground the rye by hand. I ran my fingers through the grain, removing any remaining chaff. Many of the grains were black and withered, and I picked out as many as I could. Regarding what still remained, I reminded myself that only God can truly sift and have it be complete. Once I had sufficiently ground the grain until it became flour, I was dismissed. I wish that I could have stayed for the entire process, but to be allowed to touch the holiest of holies, to aid in the creation of communion, is gift enough.

24 July, Year of Our Lord 1568

A man came to town today. An inquisitor, from the Tribunal of The Holy Office of the Inquisition. Despite the rumors that have spread through Spain about the power they hold and the quickness of their accusations, I am not worried. Father Benito met with the inquisitor and the train of traveling companions he came with, shutting themselves up in the church. I did not have time to attend tonight's prayers and inquire further about the inquisitor. Both Mamá and Papá have weakened considerably. Alonso and I are tending entirely to the farm, and it keeps us busy from dawn until dusk.

I have noticed that Alonso's hands are beginning to tremble.

28 July, Year of Our Lord 1568

The inquisitor attended Mass today. He and his brethren stood at the back of the church, watching us closely with narrowed eyes. Papá's hands have both burst open now, the over-stretched skin rupturing. I saw several of the inquisitor's men recoil, and I had to hold in a derisive snort. Mamá walked unaided for now, but her skin was pale, sweat beading on her upper lip, her eyes bright with divinity.

We found our seats, and Father Benito called us to pray. The congregation swayed, several of them collapsing to the ground in holy visions, their limbs flailing as spasms shook them. I lifted my voice in song as dark spots grew in the corners of my eyes.

Father Benito's sermon was quickly interrupted by a thundering voice, spewing hateful words about demons, devilry, and possession. The enraged inquisitor called us cursed apostates engaged in sin and blasphemy.

There were many raised voices at this, from both the townspeople and the inquisitor's cohort of men. I fell to the ground, my head pounding with the sudden noise. It was as if all the choirs of the angels of heaven and the legions of devils in hell were fighting one another, beating against the inside of my skull. I remember my mother crouching beside me, shoving communion in between my lips. It tasted mustier than usual, but I was glad for it as it strengthened my spirit enough that I was able to rise.

Alonso and Mamá grabbed me by the arms, and we moved towards the exit. There was a stampede to get out of the church as the inquisitor's men began to wade into the chaos, their weapons raised. Papá lingered behind us as we were caught up in the current of fleeing people. The last I saw him, he was screaming at the men, reaching his mangled hands towards them. One of the black-robed men raised a club, and I heard the cracking of Papá's skull before I slipped into unconsciousness.

I awoke alone in my home, curled in a ball on the hearth before a sputtering fire.

29 July, Year of Our Lord 1568

Papá is dead, his body burned with the others who were caught up in the incident at the church. Men in black cloaks are patrolling the streets, keeping us all inside. I do not know what to do besides pray.

30 July, Year of Our Lord 1568

Under armed guard, Father Benito has been escorted to the doors of the village and allowed brief entry to each household. When he came, we all held each other for a long moment as Father Benito prayed with us. He spoke with Mamá in hushed tones, and I could see her nodding her head emphatically. Afterward, Father Benito took me aside. He asked if I still wanted to travel and take my Holy Orders. I told him I had decided to stay and dedicate my life to God within the confines of my own community. He said our congregation was in peril, and that the inquisitor had told him we were all to be put on trial tomorrow, our church to be burned down regardless of the outcome. We were required to repent of our blasphemy if we wished to live. All the townsfolk thus far had refused, including Mamá; they meant to burn with the church and become martyrs.

Father Benito spoke of a dream from the previous night wherein I was given a holy mission by God Himself. I was to leave tonight and take the word of God with me to St. Joséph's, keeping the spirit of our community alive and preserving it for future generations. I begged to stay and burn with them. He said that I could not defy God's will. He pulled something from deep within his robe and shoved it into my arms, blessed me, and left.

I cannot stop weeping.

31 July, Year of Our Lord 1568

It is morning, and they are all dead. I tried to take Alonso with me. He is only eleven, but he refused; he felt called to burn. I waited until the very early hours of the morning, kissed Mamá and brother goodbye, and then slipped out through a hole in our roof, jumping down into the dust below and hurrying away. The town was crawling with the inquisitors' men, and it was only through the grace of God that I wasn't spotted. I made my way to the woods that edge our borders, and there I sat and waited. If I could not be a martyr, I could at least be a witness.

Shortly before dawn, our people trickled out slowly, the villagers assembling in front of the church. Father Benito was at the head of them as they stood awaiting their judgment. The inquisitor ordered them to repent and return to Christendom instead of the perversion they now served. He would spare the lives of all those who turned back to God and were re-baptized.

The townsfolk shuffled their feet and exchanged glances. Alonso looked up at Mamá, who laid a blackening hand on his shoulder and squeezed it. As one, the townsfolk turned and shuffled into the church, the strong aiding the weak. They had seen the face of God and had known the ecstasy of His holy fire, and they would not be turned from the truth.

Father Benito was the last one in, and he stood in the open doorway and looked out at the inquisitor and his men. Behind him, our people sang hymns, swaying to their own beats. It was a harmony without harmony, and from my hidden spot, tears begin to flood down my face at the sanctity of it all. How I wish I had been in there with them!

There was a long pause, and the inquisitor signaled to his men, and eight of them came forward bearing large barrels of pitch. They surrounded the church and began to paint and pour it on, darkening the building I held so dear. When they were finished, another eight men came forward with torches. There was a stern word from the inquisitor, and they touched their flaming ends to the black-covered walls. It ignited almost immediately.

It did not take long before the church became a funeral pyre. Screams rang out through the crackle of the flames. Black smoke billowed, and there was a great noise as the roof collapsed down into the blazing inferno. The screaming quickly stopped.

The inquisitor and his companions watched as my entire life burned. Their eyes sparked, embers smoldering in their depths. In those eyes I glimpsed hell itself—a parade of demons that leapt from person to person as they danced in victory. I looked away.

The church is still smoldering as I sit here, writing, my hands clutching the cross of Father Benito that now hangs around my neck. The sky is finally lightening, the sun painting the sky as red as blood. In my bags are our most holy relics, and several bags' worth of communion that are glowing gold and speckled with black. I will take them to Teresa and give them to her. I will take the words and wishes of our Lord to the convent, and reveal to them the truth that God has given us through the consumption of His Most Holy flesh.

This I swear.

Historian's Note: Based on the physical and psychological symptoms present in the population, it is generally believed in historical circles that the townsfolk of Deia were suffering from severe levels of ergot poisoning. Ergot, a fungus found primarily on rye and transmitted via airborne spores, causes schizophrenic-like delusions, hallucinations, sepsis, and body degradation. Furthermore, its effects have been known to cause religious mania when ingested.

Some academics have hypothesized that many of those killed during the Inquisition and later witch trials were suffering from some form of ergot poisoning.

THAW

With the night came the dead.

Samuel stoked the fire and held his bolt-action rifle close to his chest. The wind shrieked and rattled the windows, pushing the bitter cold through minuscule gaps in the log cabin walls. He watched the flames lick at the wood and huddled closer, wondering how much longer it would be until they arrived.

He didn't have to wait long. Barely a quarter of an hour had passed when he heard the first knock against the door. It was probably *her* knocking, and he wondered if her pack was close behind her. Both his throat and his grip on the rifle tightened, knuckles whitening. He waited.

She had been the first one to arrive, six days past. It had been close to midnight when someone rapped at the door, startling him out of his slumber. It hadn't snowed that night, and so when Samuel looked out the window to see who could have made the trek to his cabin at such a late hour, he could see her standing there, her silhouette dark against the moonlight. Her dress was stiff with ice. An arm, bare and withered, knocked on the door. She turned from the door to face the window, allowing him to see her horrible face.

It was long and lean, the cheekbones jutting prominently from sunken cheeks. Her skin was dry and browned, mottled, as if it had turned to leather during the mummification process. Her lips were still in evidence. They were round and surprisingly full, pulled back in a terrible, never-ending smile. One of her front teeth was missing. Her long dark hair was caked in ice crystals, hanging heavily down to her waist in a frosty curtain.

She shuffled over to the window, one leg dragging behind her, far thinner and withered than the other. She leaned in close. Her nose might have been pert once, maybe even cute, but now it was black and frostbitten, the winter cold having eaten away at it. She tilted her head as if she had seen him, despite there being two gaping holes in her face in the place of eyes, the rims of them dry and neat. He stood transfixed, his cheek pressed against the frosty window.

Samuel jerked back as she laid long, brittle, spidery fingers against the glass. She tapped each finger, one at a time, slowly at first, speeding up as her knuckles cracked and regained the movement that had been lost to them. She stood there, tapping, tapping, tapping, teeth bared, as he slowly backed away.

He felt like he might throw up. His heart was in his throat, and it choked him. His mind stuttered over words and feelings, stuck on repeat: *What is that what is that WHAT IS THAT*. For a long time, the two of them remained there, trapped in a surreal stalemate, one of them tapping and asking for entrance, and one of them refusing to answer.

A log popped in the fire, and the spell broke. He lunged towards the wall where his rifle hung, loaded and ready, then bounded across the cabin and threw open the door, swinging the rifle up.

An empty night greeted him. The dark sky was peppered by stars, the moon bright and full and hanging low in the sky, illuminating his property. His yard was empty, save for the old corn and kale stalks in his garden jutting up out of the snow like the spears of a buried army. He carefully searched his land, but she was gone. All that remained of the woman were her footprints—one set leading towards his cabin, and one set leading away into the naked woods. He didn't sleep but stood guard for the entire night.

In the morning, even those footprints were gone, the snow melting just enough to obscure where she had disturbed it. He knew where she had come from though, and he avoided that part of the woods as he trudged through them, checking his traplines. The animals were already leaving their winter dens, and he found some success with a few squirrels. Back at the cabin, he skinned them and made a lean meat stew along with a few withered potatoes. He devoured it quickly, standing in the open doorway of his home, watching the woods. He puttered around the cabin for a few more hours, and when the sun began to set, he braced himself for her return.

The next night, she came at the stroke of midnight, and she didn't come alone.

Samuel watched through the icy window as she dragged her withered leg behind her. She had made it more than halfway to his front door when a larger, darker shape emerged from the woods behind her.

It was a man—or had been once. He was not as badly decomposed as she was; his skin was an ashy shade of blue instead of frost-bitten black. His eyes were still present, a horrible shade of brilliant blue, though unfocused. His face seemed wrong, his features hanging as if they had been squashed. He didn't limp but staggered. His shock of red hair was half on end, and half terribly matted and dusted with snow and dirt. Mud streaked his skin. His pants were half soaked, half frozen. One foot was bare, and on the other was a stained and filthy hand-sewn boot.

As he drew nearer, Samuel saw that his head was half-caved in. Pieces of skull jutted out at odd angles from the crater that had been the top of his cranium. Bits of frozen brain splattered his forehead. His strange eyes stayed fixed on the door of the cabin, and Samuel couldn't help but panic as the pair drew closer.

"Go away!" he said, banging on the window. The two bodies turned towards him. "Get the hell out of here!"

They came to the window, and the woman began her tap-tap-tapping again. The man just stood there for a moment before turning back to the door. Clumsy hands grasped at the handle, and the door rattled for a moment. The woman ceased her tapping and with those empty eye sockets, looked towards her companion. As if they had spoken to one another in a language he could not hear, they turned back to the woods and began the same shuffle-step. After a few minutes, they disappeared into the forest of the Colorado mountains.

The whole episode lasted less than ten minutes but left Samuel exhausted. He collapsed onto his bunk, still holding his rifle. He slept fitfully, with dreams of the man and the woman holding him down as a bush knife carved into his flesh. He woke up screaming with the dawn.

The traps were empty that day, and his stomach growled. He thought of the things that had visited him, and that stilled it. Better to lose one's appetite than to deal with the pangs of it, he thought. Neater that way, and certainly less troublesome.

The third night, there came a spring blizzard. He waited up by the window for the entire night, but the sleeting snow made it hard to see more than a foot, and it must have been the same for his visitors. He dozed off just as the storm died down and the windows began to brighten.

When he awoke, it was already mid-afternoon, and he knew he had to rush down to the town for his weekly appointment to sell the few scraggly pelts he had that were worth selling.

"Looks like you aren't sleeping well," Alonzo said from across the counter of the small, dark general store. A sad candle wavered, barely bolstering the weak spring light that filtered in through the front window. Alonzo's dark eyes peered at Samuel, and in response Samuel pulled his hat down further over his eyes.

"Not," Samuel said gruffly. "But t'ain't none of your business."

Alonzo raised his hands. "No offense intended. Just wanted to check in. We have to take care of one another. It was a hard winter, and it looks like spring will be no better. That Welsh boy is still missing, and several of my shipments of non-perishables haven't shown up. People are starting to get hungry."

Samuel grunted. "I'm sure he'll turn up."

Alonzo smiled weakly. "We can pray." He extended his hand, which rattled with a few small coins. "Here. For the furs."

Samuel held out his large, chapped hand. Alonzo dropped them in, and Samuel shoved them into his pocket. Neither of them acknowledged that the paltry sum was not enough for Samuel to buy anything. Alonzo just watched as Samuel turned around without another word.

It was nearly sunset when Samuel left town, and he urged his feet to move faster home. The sun sank beneath the treetops and the shadows lengthened. Light snow crunched beneath his feet. The temperature dropped, and his beard and whiskers began to freeze with the condensation from his breath. The sounds of the forest seemed muffled, and the dark sky pressed down on him. He felt intensely claustrophobic, and before he knew it, he was jogging.

He crossed onto his property, and as he approached the door, a twig snapped behind him and he whirled. Fifty feet away, he saw them. This time, the woman and the man with the skull wound lingered as two new figures made their way in his direction, speeding up as they saw him. It was a dark-haired man and woman, similar in appearance.

The dark-haired man, with his strong profile and his broken and badly healed nose, had a large gunshot wound in his stomach. He hunched over as he walked, his hands stained dark red as he held his intestines in as he moved. A length of them dripped out from between his fingers and dangled there. His face was pulled back and frozen in a horrible scowl.

His companion, a short woman with the same dark skin and flashing eyes in a round face, also had a gunshot wound, though in the middle of her chest. Her ribs were shattered, her chest caved in underneath her buckskin. Their eyes were fixed on Samuel, and they moved far quicker than the other two had. Though expressionless, from them emanated a sense of such malice that Samuel nearly froze in place from the strength of it. He bolted for the door and barely managed to slam it in place before the four of them were there, tapping on the window and rattling the handle. The second woman peered in through the other window.

"I have no quarrel with you," he said in a whisper to the assembled corpses, his massive bulk trembling. "There is no help for you here." They continued to scrabble at the glass and door, and the dark-haired man and woman went around the side of the cabin. He could hear them there, just on the other side of the wall, pacing. He let out a moan and curled onto his bed.

When he woke before dawn, the yard was empty and he was alone again. His eyes burned. He dug into an old chest filled with tattered clothing, bits and bobs, bent bullet casings. At the very bottom of it, wrapped in an oilskin, was his father's old Bible.

He took it out and carefully laid it on his bed. He was not a learned man—he could do basic reading and writing but had never been partial to religion. Sure, he knew and had attended church here and there, but staring at the Bible made him feel like a child again, visiting a house that was not his own. He flipped through its worn pages gingerly and wondered if it could help him.

His stomach rumbled and he went out and cut the branches off of a pine tree and brewed them into a tea. It was astringent, but the bitter water helped settle his stomach somewhat. It had been weeks since he'd eaten anything of substance, and he felt himself growing weaker. The issues with the reanimated dead needed to end, and soon.

That night, he stood at the front door, the Bible held in his hand. Five figures stood at the edge of the woods, and when they realized he had seen them, they moved towards him purposefully. His eyes caught on the new figure.

She had been blonde once, but her hair was so matted with mud and filth that he could barely tell. Her face was slack, and her pretty blue dress was stained down the front from where her blood had spilled from a slice so deep and wide across her throat that she was nearly decapitated.

Samuel held the Bible up like a shield. "Be gone!" he bellowed. "Be gone in the name of God!" He couldn't help but tremble. The five of them paused for a moment, heads tilting like dogs, and he felt a moment of hope. "In the name of the Father, the Son, and the Holy Spirit!"

They started towards him again, slowly, methodically. He shouted at them again and again, but it wasn't until the new woman was only ten feet away and began to reach out a pale arm towards him that his courage faltered and he dove inside, slamming the door just as they reached his cabin and began their nightly torture.

Samuel lay where he had fallen, the Bible clutched to his chest, and cried all night.

Now it was the sixth night, and the woman rapped against the door before she moved to the window, her fingers beating against it like his heart beat against his ribs, fluttering in fear and in rage. He had draped the windows so the dead could not peer in, nor could he look out upon them. He knew without a doubt who would be joining them tonight, and when he closed his eyes, Samuel could envision every detail.

It would be a man, dressed in tattered old mining clothes, his face streaked with soot and holes worn in his boots. He was missing several teeth, but only one of those was on Samuel's conscience. His hair would be long and snarled, his beard ragged and filled with detritus from both pre and post burial. His jaw would hang loosely, the right side of it shattered from when Samuel's left fist had plowed into it, and both eyes would be black. He'd bear a broken left arm and a dislocated shoulder. Samuel wondered if the corpse would cradle it, or whether it hung limply by his side as he approached the house. So vividly he could picture it that he barely jumped when the door began to rattle with increased force, and both windows were being knocked against so loudly that he feared they would break. Samuel sat by the fire, despairingly listening to the corpses as they sought entry to his cabin and to him.

He wished he had some whiskey, but he had not had so much as a burning sip since coming across the tramp, insensible on the outskirts of town, collapsed in a bush just off the trail that led to Samuel's cabin.

They were out there all night, waiting for him. He never moved from his chair before the fire, just stared at his hands and wondered if it had truly been worth it. By the time the tapping, rapping, and scratching sounds faded, he came to a decision.

He spent the day sleeping, and when he woke, he boiled the last of his small potatoes. He ate them in three bites, and then when the water he'd boiled them in cooled, he gulped that down as well. His stomach gnawed at itself.

Tonight would be the last night. The final one, the freshest one. The Welsh boy. He stood on the threshold of his cabin, rifle in his hands. *Let the dead come*, he thought to himself. Let them see what he was made of. He planted his feet, as firm as an oak tree, and waited.

They came when the moon had barely risen above the treetops. He raised his rifle to his shoulder and shot it. The red-haired man came through first, and he staggered back with the force of the bullet, falling backwards into the mud. From the woods around him, similar shadows emerged as the red-headed man struggled back upright, a visible gaping wound in his chest, dry and ragged and completely inconsequential.

"I killed you all once, and I'll kill you all again!" Samuel roared in challenge. "Leave me be!" He reloaded, his fingers fumbling with the bolt. He raised it and fired, this time at the short dark-haired woman. Half of her face exploded away, but she barely staggered back.

Again and again he fired as they continued their procession, his shots growing wider. When they reached him, they stood in a half-circle ten feet from the door. He was out of bullets. Dropping the rifle, he put out his hands beseechingly to the corpses.

"What do you want?" he said hoarsely, scanning their faces. Guilt was an anchor on his soul, and his knees threatened to buckle. "What do you want from me?"

They stared at him with their dead eyes. It was the warmest night yet, and the ice that had coated their heads dripped down their cheeks like tears as it melted, glistening in the waning moonlight. At their feet, small puddles formed as their tattered, wet clothes clung to them, no longer obscuring the pieces that the starving Samuel had carved away from them over the course of the winter. A cut of thigh there, a pair of missing breasts, a filleted chest—all of them exposed in the wet warmth of spring. Then they parted, and the smallest member of their party came forward, the crimes of the winter revealed in his young flesh.

The Welsh boy stood naked at the front of the group, barely coming up to the hulking Samuel's waist, and stared up at him with eyes so glazed they were opaque. His arms and legs were skeletal, boiled and soft, with teeth marks scraped into the bone. His thighs had been carved away, and his shirt clung to an empty and emaciated torso. The wound underneath his ribs, the careful cut where Samuel had reached in with his oversized fingers to remove the tender organs, still somehow oozed. The boy craned his neck as he met Samuel's eyes and he reached out one skeletal hand to slip it into Samuel's hand, the same way he had when Samuel had promised to show him his traplines on the day when the two of them had accidentally met in the snowy woods. His bones were cold. Samuel could see the necklace of bruises around the boy's throat, a chain of black and purple.

"I'm sorry, I'm so sorry," Samuel sobbed. "I was hungry, I was just so hungry."

The boy tugged on his hand, and the lion followed the lamb out to the middle of the yard. Once they were away from the cabin, the Welsh boy let go of him and stepped back.

The rest of them fell upon him, and Samuel screamed.

LAID BARE

SHE IS YOUNGER than him, but not so much younger that his interest falls into outright predation. His intentions are not noble, but in his opinion they don't need to be so long as they fall within the letter of the law. He is careful, always careful, to toe that line.

He finds her in the chatboard of an almost defunct art website and is intrigued by her profile picture. When he clicks through, he finds that it is a self-portrait. In it, she is nude, her delicate face pointing upwards as she stares at a shimmering sky of strangely coloured stars and auroras twisting like snakes.

It's only when he zooms in to look at her naked body that he realizes she's holding something. She is clutching a blanket that is wrapped around her like a robe. It is painted as if it were her body, and her hands draw it tight against her curves. It is skillfully done, and the reveal that isn't quite a reveal arousing. It is a promise, a temptation, a tantalizing tease that puts a question mark in the mind of the viewer, and he has *many* questions.

He slides like a snake into her messages, praises her technique in the way he knows women love. She doesn't take long to respond.

"Thank you. I'm Annie. Who are you?"

It is a whirlwind internet romance. They exchange thousands of messages, and after a week of the back and forth, she calls him on the phone. Her voice is tentative and trembling, and it excites him in a way that he hasn't been in a very long time. Desire pools in his stomach and drips silver beads out the end of his cock. They pool in the hollow of his stomach as he strokes himself to the sound of her breathy voice.

They talk into the early hours of the morning. Afterwards, he stands outside smoking on his condo balcony and wonders if he is the first she has ever talked to like that—if he will be her first. He hopes he is.

He plies her with nonsense, empty words and snatches of poetry he's stolen from the internet. He sends her flowers. She hasn't given him her address, so he sends it to the place where she gets her morning coffee. She calls him after, eager and excited. She's never received flowers before. The way she thanks him has warmth pooling in his chest and groin. It distracts him from his work, and he finds himself ducking into the office bathroom for a quick release, her name on his lips.

She paints him a picture of how he makes her feel, sends him a grainy photo of it—as his eyes roam over it. He can admit that she really is good. He tells her he is going to print it out and frame it and then deletes the file from his phone like all the others.

After a while, his pleas to meet are met with less stony resistance, less hesitancy. He slathers it on thick, buttering her up like a breakfast toast. Finally, she tells him of a restaurant she knows and loves; they can meet there next week. He can barely keep the lust out of his voice when he agrees.

He arrives early, watches the door like a hawk. When she finally shows up, her makeup is demure, her shoulder-length blonde hair down and brushed back behind her ears. He watches the thin strap of her light pink dress slip down her shoulder, her slender fingers righting it in a self-conscious manner as she approaches the table. She looks delicious. He salivates and flags down the waiter, never once taking his eyes off of her.

He woos her over a bottle of Pinot Noir and fish tacos. By the end of the date, the walls he could see in her eyes when she arrived have fallen entirely, leaving her defenseless. She begins to tell him everything about herself, her deepest thoughts, her dreams and fears. He wants to ask her about her desires and resists the urge to seduce her right there and then.

He drums his fingers against his leg impatiently, imagines running them up her thighs instead. He wants to slide them underneath the elastic of her panties and sink them into her wet warmth.

He pays the bill, and when she pauses outside the restaurant, he gives her a single chaste kiss on her smooth and unblemished cheek and bids her goodnight. He begins to walk away, his chest painfully aware of her presence, his ears straining in hopes she will say the words he wants to hear. Dinner had not even begun to whet his appetite. He hopes she takes the bait.

She does.

"Does it have to be goodnight? The night is still young—I know a place down the road." Her voice is full of false confidence that makes him chuckle before he turns around.

He pays for the motel in cash—it wouldn't do for his wife to know his business dinner is for business of a different sort. As she fidgets next to him, she stares up at him with eager eyes lightly filmed by lust and trepidation. When he slides the key into the lock of the door and twists it, she begins to tremble. He wraps his arm around her and draws her inside, closing the door firmly behind them and locking it.

He kisses her slowly at first, his tongue probing for entrance. She melts into his arms. Her hands travel over his hard chest, and he reaches up to cup a soft breast. She moans into his mouth, and he pulls back for a moment, wanting to savor his conquest. She is young, so very young, and he has so much to teach her.

He goes to remove her dress, barely holding back the ravenous beast that strains inside him. He wants to throw her down and thrust himself into her, wants to bite and to tear, but he must be patient. She stops him with a shaking hand, a touch of fear stealing into her eyes. It makes him want her more.

Her token resistance means nothing to him, so he crushes her to him. She smells like a garden, an innocent blush of roses undercut with lilac and sweetpea. He kisses insistently up her neck as she arches it back with a greedy whimper.

"I love everything about you," he coos into her ear, pressing a kiss against her earlobe in the same way his hardness presses against her thighs. "I think you're my person, Annie."

"Really?" she whispers, and there is such a crushing vulnerability and a tentative hope there that he has to stifle the groan of need building in his chest so that he doesn't frighten her off and things end before they have even begun.

"I want to know all of your secrets," he says. "I want you laid bare before me."

She thinks he means one thing; he definitely means another. He doesn't bother to correct her.

"Okay. Let me then," she says, pulling back. He lets go of her reluctantly, takes a step back to undress himself. He lies back on the rumpled bedding of the motel to watch her, naked and ready.

She stands at the end of the bed, her eyes hungrily taking him in, following the lines of his body down to land between his legs. His cock is harder, harder than it's ever felt. His desire is agony.

"Please," he begs her. "I want to see you. All of you."

She surrenders. This time when she slides her fingers under the strap of her dress, she is not shy about it. He sees smooth, white skin, traces his eyes along the dip of her collarbone and swell of her hips. He doesn't bother to stifle a groan as her body becomes fully exposed, the pink dress falling to the threadbare carpet in surrender.

She stands there, the ghost of a smile on her face. He sits up and reaches towards her, his hands curling into claws in his desperation to drag her into the bed and own her.

"I'm not finished yet," she says shyly. "Don't you want to see all of me?"

Her hands reach up to the back of her neck, and she starts tearing. She peels away her skin, her bloodless flesh opening up like a great and terrible flower. Something black and shiny, segmented like the carapace of a beetle, becomes visible as she shells off her exterior, dropping it to the ground like an old flesh-coloured curtain next to her dress.

She is a thousand things and more—a giant centipede, a million ants coalesced together, an incomprehensible swirling of shadow and stars. She is the nightmare creature lurking in his childhood closet, the cold draft that slides under the cellar door. He can barely comprehend any or all of her. He stifles a scream and pulls back his hands as if burned.

"Do you still want me?" she warbles at him. Her words are like a thousand voices at once, all overlaid so that her throat is like a crowd lovingly murmuring at him.

He throws up in his mouth, crawls away until his back presses against the stained headboard, banging it against the wall. Her eyes are black pools, and he stares into them while his cock falls limp against his muscled thigh. She seems to take his silence as an assent, beams with many sharp smiles, teeth clacking together in delight and anticipation.

"That's what I thought," she says with delight. Her black eyes, all of them, flutter at him and with the gentle movement of a thousand delicate legs like tree roots, she scuttles up onto the bed. There is nowhere he can run, nowhere he can hide. He is frozen, the dirty light from the window falling across him, boxing him in so that he can't move. "I knew you loved me, knew as soon as I met you we were meant to be, that you would be my first."

Her thoraxes pulse with excitement as she rears over him and then lowers herself down gently, wrapping the largest two of her appendages around him like arms. They crawl across his skin like great white slugs as they caress him. He can feel them probing, the sharp edges sliding underneath his skin and lingering there, as if sipping at his blood. Tears leak from his eyes, and he begins to shiver and shake.

"Please," he says. "*Please.*"

"Of course, my darling," she replies, and presses her black and bloated lips, all twelve of them, against his bare skin. "I love you."

He screams and writhes as she begins to consume him, each small bite as soft and tender as any kiss.

The Madness of Mermaids

It begins with a drip, an echoing what-if ringing through your skull. It is relentless, eroding away your sanity as you glide through the deep and the dark. *Drip. Drip. Drip.* Whatever it is, it is ancient and cruel. Unceasing, it offers no reprieve.

You can't place it for a while. It is slow and steady, like grains of sand in an hourglass, as it slides down into you. Not until you are half-full with a sea of your own do you recognize it for what it is—longing. It is the songs of those who swam before you reflecting off of the reefs, a history of misery amplified through waves and water. It crashes into you, and you are flooded with feeling. You *want*.

You know how it will end, how it always ends, but that doesn't stop you from trying. You move to the shallows near the shoreline. Your tail splits and your gills close up and you take in that first dry gasp of air. It tastes like a desert, fills your lungs with smoldering embers. You stumble through hot sand, the loneliness driving you on despite the pain. You already miss the water.

You see him there, walking along the shore, and follow him. You are a siren, so when he sees you, he sees what so many have seen before: temptation. You give yourself willingly, and when you both are finished, he

falls asleep in the calm cove of your arms. His breath is hypnotic, the gentle shush of waves lapping against the shore. There are constellations in the freckles on his face. You wonder if you can navigate by them; you wonder if you are home.

Time passes. That fire, that frenzy of passion where two people crash together with all the violence of an oceanic storm, begins to dim. He tells you once that the sand is worn down rock and shell, a graveyard accumulated over centuries. Dead things are deposited there; no wonder everything hurts now, when you were also washed up with them by the tide.

You are awash in him—in hope, in love, in faith that this time is the right time. Your ferocity is lost as you allow yourself to be encompassed. You sink into him as you would into the water. You are tossed and turned within him, shapely driftwood made less sharp. You tell yourself that the growing lack of movement between you two is not an omen. It is just the soft sinking of sediment as things settle.

Soon you can't ignore him drifting away. *Love me, love me, love me,* you call after him as you follow his fading footsteps along the place where the ocean kisses the shore. You keep following him until his passion turns to sullenness. The waters between you grow murkier. One day, he finally tells you it's over, the pearls of his words turning to razor clams as they drip from his lips. The tide has gone out, and yet you still feel as though you are bogged down and drowning. He looks at you with shark's eyes and you wonder how you managed to fall for it again; it seems this is a lesson you refuse to learn.

You taste the salt of your tears and on your lips. It reminds you of yourself, of the furious fathoms that churn within you. Something else fills you then besides love, something raging and primeval. You find yourself reaching into his chest like the predator you are. You rip out his heart, and you eat it, biting into it as if it were an overripe fruit. Its juice floods your mouth, dripping down your chin and staining your hands like henna. As you devour it, the dam within bursts and any love remaining flows out of you.. You become hollow, nothing but a great empty scar in the landscape. You are a shipwreck on the seabed, an empty vessel populated only by ghosts.

You feast upon all that remains of what was once your love, but you are still empty. You return to the sea hoping it will fill you up again. And it does—it always does. You will lie in a bed of soothing soft kelp and recover, sharpening your teeth against oyster shells. Eventually, the trickle will begin again, turn to a wave, turn to a tsunami that washes away any vestigial pain and drives you back to land. You will poke your head over the top of the restless waters to look up at the mountains silhouetted against the moon, and marvel at the vastness of the sky. You will crawl across the rocks, your new legs throbbing, and go hunting again.

Like the wild and desperate sea, you do not subscribe to logic, but you do succumb to predictability.

A CATHEDRAL IN HER CHEST

MAGDA KNOWS AS soon as the transformation begins. She sits at the back of the church, alone except for an old man who lights a candle and bows his head to pray before it. The pew is cold and hard, but she doesn't notice. She stares at the cross hung behind the altar and pinches her knuckles, one by one, as she repeats her Hail Marys.

Je vous salue, Marie, pleine de grâce.

Her father has taken her rosary away. *As punishment*, he said, *for killing your mother. For all your sins. I hope you die too.* Magda just bowed her head and remained silent, though the loss of her rosary hurt deeply. She's learned to accept her father's words. He is always getting into a mood. Her head bows now, too, lips exhaling tiny vapours in the cold air. The church has not yet heated up—it is very early in the morning, and she can faintly hear the rattling cough of the ancient furnace as it struggles to come alive. No matter. She is used to the cold.

She places the pew rail down gingerly and kneels. A soft sigh escapes her lips. The cushioned rail is much softer than the wooden floors at home, where she has knelt for hours, in prayer and penance for her father. Her

knees are bruised, scraped, and bleeding, and she shifts to a slightly more comfortable position and tries to focus on the Truth instead of the pain.

Magda is becoming a cathedral. For months she has felt her transformation brewing in the pit of her. Her prayers grow more fervent. She wishes for nothing more than to settle on a deep foundation, down on the rock of Saint Peter with a creak and a groan, and to open her doors to a spiritually hungry populace. To be of use. She fingers the crude cross she has made into a necklace with a bit of string.

Le Seigneur est avec vous.

You are a fool, her father screams when she tells him, *an idiot as the day you were born. People do not become churches. God does not love you enough to make you a church.* He raises his fist then, and Magda closes her eyes. After, he drags her bleeding back to her own room and abandons her naked above the sheets. He leaves the window open, snowflakes flying in to settle on her skin like heavenly kisses.

Magda whispers another prayer. It would not do to think unkindly of her father. The priest has not yet entered the confessional, and she can not confess. A sin so heavy should not blemish her like that. *Little whore*, her father hisses in her mind. She pushes down the memory and stares at the Bible in front of her.

Vous êtes bénie entre toutes les femmes,

She can feel something quickening inside of her. It fills her with trepidation bordering on ecstasy. She thinks of Saint Teresa, of holy fire and transformation. She looks at the faces of angels on the frescoes on the wall and presses her hands together. One of her fingers is broken, but she doesn't feel it. She feels expectant.

Her ribs became like timbers, groaning and stretching. They press up and out, hindering her breath. She grows round and radiant, but a sibilant hiss escapes unwillingly. It hurts. A choir hums in her bones, accompanied by the gentle murmur of the waiting congregation. Their footsteps echo through her belly. *Saint Marie, please, please make me a chapel worthy of God.*

et Jésus, le fruit de vos entrailles, est béni.

The man at the altar looks up. She nods to him, keeping her eyes downcast.

Her skin stretches, and a sudden cramp has her falling from the railing to lie in the aisle. The old man gets up, hesitantly taking a few steps closer.

Mademoiselle? Mademoiselle, are you alright? She does not move, so he comes closer. *Mademoiselle, your face, my God your face. Are you alright?* Magda winces and raises a hand to cover her face. She knows that she is ugly, uglier than usual. Her face is bruised and beaten. Blood trickles from a small cut on her temple.

I am alright, she says. *It is nothing.* He leans forward to help her up. She cries when she accidentally puts weight on her broken ankle. Inside her, the cathedral swells, pushes up and out. Her belly ripples.

Mademoiselle you are in labour, the man exclaims. He is panicking, wrinkled hands pulling at thinning hair.

No, she tries to tell them, *there is a cathedral in my chest,* but he pushes her down and does not listen.

The baby is coming. I don't have a cell phone. Where is your family?

He has left me here, my father, she tries to explain. *He is angry with me. I am to atone. I am a sinner.*

You are a mother, the old man replies.

Sainte Marie, Mère de Dieu,

No, no, I am to be a church.

The man is gently laying her down. She can feel the pressure of the cathedral inside of her. She is so close.

The man lifts her skirt. Panic overwhelms her. She pushes it back down. No, no. There is something wrong with this, she knows. She cannot put her finger on it. For a second, she sees her father there and tastes blood in her mouth. Panic. The old man tries to soothe her. *Hush. Hush. The baby, the baby.*

There is no baby, she knows this. There is only a soaring ceiling with stained glass windows like blue eyes, and the glowing of the candles shining out her skin. She can feel herself unfolding, but the old man rips her skirt. There is pressure, so much pressure. She never thought it would hurt this much.

I will be right back, the man says. He runs for the altar, grabs a chalice and dips it in the font before he pauses and rips the altar cloth off of it. The silver dishes and candlesticks clatter to the floor. A candle gutters out. *No, no don't do that,* Magda wants to cry, but she is so thirsty. The man rushes back. He is carrying the altar cloth. He bundles it beneath her outstretched legs, puts the goblet to her lips. She tastes water, holy and sweet.

Priez pour nous, pauvres pécheurs

I can see the head.

There is no head. There are pews and goblets and hosts.

Push, please, push. The baby's face is blue.

There is no baby, but she can feel the cathedral ready to explode out of her, send spires hurtling skywards, and pushes anyway.

One more, mademoiselle, one more, you are almost there.

With a prayer on her lips, dry and chapped and cracked, she heaves again and she splits in two, the cathedral rushing up and out, through her chest and through her groin, growing and spreading with an intense and searing heat. She screams once, and then falls back.

It is a boy, the old man says, *it is a boy. But the blood, oh god, the blood. Mademoiselle, please, mademoiselle can you hear me? The baby is not moving. Mademoiselle? Please, Mademoiselle, stay with me.*

maintenant et à l'heure de notre mort.

I can hear you, she wants to say. But the words don't come. Her body shudders. She feels light, lighter than air. She is a prayer, floating, floating, high into the rafters, singing joy, a wordless hymn that she knows pleases her Father. She sinks into the stones of the walls, into the altar and the candles.

Amen.

Below, tears are drying on battered cheeks, and an old man is weeping.

In the Footsteps of Ghosts

Note; The following written account was found in the desk of the Marquess _________ of ___________________, following his apparent suicide at the age of ____.

If you were to enter Braşov Forest, just west of the town of Braşov in the shadows of the Carpathian Mountains, you would find yourself in a primeval place. It is a forest of deep shadows, rocky terrain, and tall dark pines crowded together so thickly there is barely space for a man to squeeze in between them. If you were to continue down small and meandering roads where humanity has made weak attempts to reach the heart of the forest, you would hear rustling as unseen creatures move through the underbrush, and you would always have the sense of being watched, as if there were a malicious presence tracking you through the dark. It is a desolate place, where the very air is so oppressive that it threatens to push you down, deep into the black loam, with its sheer weight.

When I left my father's house to travel for a summer, I resolved to do as much as I could without the benefit of his wealth, in order to experience the true culture of the cities I would visit along my pre-planned route. I was determined to have "the authentic experience". Thus far, the authentic experience has been filled with small cots brimming with insect life and questionable stains, cold and rainy afternoons spent plodding towards my next destination, and perhaps the ingestion of a little too much laudanum at the end of particularly bitter days when my muscles cramped unceasingly and my hands became so cold they curled into claws.

Still, I was stubborn, and told myself that when I returned to the plush comforts of my everyday life, I would have a strength of character that the majority of my coddled peers would not possess, as well as many scandalous stories that would titillate and impress both my friends in the gentry and the fairer sex. I used my father's money only for supplies, and once for the sake of a very hot bath filled with perfumed oils, followed by a massage by a rather well-endowed woman speaking in such a heavy accent I couldn't understand her, though I could certainly understand her hands.

Alas, she was many cities away, and as I stood at the edge of the forest, the hairs along my arms rose. I would never say that precognition was on my list of notable skills, but something at that moment told me I was about to enter the unknown, and it filled me with a thrilling trepidation. The mountain winds blew rather fiercely, but the thick wall of trees barely showed any movement, and I began to wonder if my desire to visit the Brașov Fort was perhaps an unwise one.

I had planned to visit the fort since before I'd left England, and its history was as long and as dark as any I had ever read, and it had fascinated me for as long as I'd known about it. Centuries ago, it had been the stronghold of a local warlord who, as the legends went, had been driven mad by greed and lust for power and began to attack and lay siege to the surrounding area, amassing an enormous army of cutthroat mercenaries. Known for his viciousness and cruelty, he'd been a thorn in Eastern Europe's side for over twenty years. While he didn't have quite the historical pull that despots such as Vlad Tempes or Genghis Khan carried, he was a fascinating figure in his own right.

It wasn't until several of his alliances formed their own secret alliance after a failed negotiation that his campaign for domination ended, following one long night brimming with blood and betrayal. When the sun rose, the warlord had not been there to see it. Upon one of his own pennant poles, his head had been mounted, eyes gouged out and tongue removed, empty sockets gazing toward the dark expanse of Braşov forest. I've heard it whispered his head stayed there for several months until one of the storms the area was known for had snapped the pole, sending the skull tumbling down into the forest where it was never recovered. I had half a mind to look for the skull—what a memento that would make!—but knew I could not afford the time it would take to comb through the brush in the search for what might end up being nothing more than a bedtime story.

I had with me my trusty walking stick, a pack filled with worn clothes, and bruised, soggy food. I had stopped to refill some of my supplies that morning—a new oilskin tarp that could be used for both shelter and blankets depending on how clear the night was, some extra rope, and a new flint. At the bottom of my bag was a false bottom, and packed into it was a large amount of different currencies, as well as a full bottle of potent laudanum I'd procured at a rather seedy-looking apothecary.

When I eventually mustered my nerve and entered the woods, it was with nothing but my own hubris to keep me company. I was determined to conquer the Braşov forest on my own and find my way to the fort. As I traveled along the overgrown road—which had been reduced to nothing more than a worn path—I hummed to myself, confident I could reach the fort without aid.

The first two days were monotonous, and I often felt like I barely made any progress. The terrain was difficult to traverse, and in many places the path disappeared entirely. I had to survey the growth of the forest around me and follow the youngest of the trees and the bushes that obstructed my way to find the road again. My legs were so sore they trembled as I walked. I refused to give up and turn around, struggling onwards toward my goal instead. Perhaps I'd miscalculated the time and provisions needed to reach the crumbling fort, as well as my own physical strength, because I quickly found myself burning through the food and potable water I'd brought. I found some cool, clear springs to refresh my waterskin, but eating was going to quickly become an issue. With me was a small book on wilderness survival, but with some chagrin I realized I had forgotten the supplies needed to construct basic traps. I would have to figure something else out.

Even if I had the necessary items, I'm not sure it would have done much good. Despite the lushness of the greenery and the constant feeling that I was being observed, I did not see much beyond a few crows and stringy squirrels. Larger animal life never revealed itself to me, and I saw no sign of them.

On the third day, it rained. The fort, perched high upon a craggy hill, finally came into view to the left of my position. Reorienting myself, I clambered towards it, the raised elevation slowing me. I had hoped to make it there before nightfall and camp within its crumbled walls, but in the early afternoon it began to drizzle. I continued onward, soaked to the skin and chilled, my burning muscles providing no warmth to the rest of me. Thick droplets dripped down the hanging pine branches, and no matter how carefully I moved, I would inevitably brush against something that would send a shower raining down on me. I was cold, I was miserable, and I swore heartily under my breath as the sun set and the already shadowy forest began to darken. I would not make it to the fort by the end of the day.

I attempted to set up camp on the decrepit road that night underneath the low-hanging boughs of a gargantuan pine. My fire was small and sputtered, going out often, leaving me to huddle underneath my blanket, taking generous swings of the laudanum. It falsely warmed me, and a sense of euphoria washed over me as my body relaxed. The pain in my muscles began to dissipate, my eyes becoming half-lidded, the world blurring as the narcotic and alcohol's effects took a firm and blissful hold. My eyes drifted shut and, despite the misery of my surroundings, in no time at all I fell asleep.

I was plunged immediately into a nightmare, a lucid dream so indistinguishable from reality that it was as if I were still awake and sitting at the dying campfire. An unseen battle raged around me, the grunts and moans and screams of dying men filling the air, which was so thick with the stench of sweat and death that I could taste the iron tang of blood on my tongue. At first there was nothing visible—just the sounds of crashing branches and the fury of men at war. Slowly but surely, as if the men were fading from their world into this one, the outline of bodies appeared. They were like ghosts at first—I could see the vegetation through them—but they began to solidify as the battle intensified.

It wasn't long before I was caught in the middle of a chaotic battlefield. Men died around me, their screams echoing through the woods. The ground was soaked with blood. Somewhere, I could smell wood-smoke and something rancid burning, which I could only assume was the scent of cooking human flesh.

There was a heavy grunt and a horrible rending noise, and a head rolled down to rest at my feet. Long black hair pulled back in a rough braid framed a face with a square jaw and a thick, coarse beard. Eyes too small and beady for the rough-hewn face stared up at me from overtop a crooked, jagged nose. The irises were black as sin and would have blended in entirely with the pupil if it weren't for the dim fire that burned within them. It was as if they were windows into a raging inferno that sparked and flickered. Thick lips pulled back from sharpened teeth as it began to decay at an advanced rate, the skin festering and rotting, the muscle beneath sliding wetly off of the skull as it putrefied. The bone itself began to shift and to grow. Long antlers like those of a pronghorn deer erupted from the forehead; the teeth grew longer until the size of them forced open the jaw. The cheekbones grew sharper, elongating with the jawbone, and when the eyes rolled back into the sockets and down into the skull, the fire continued to burn within the pits—twin flames that reminded me of Sundays spent at church, the priest thundering at the pulpit about hellfire and damnation. I became a small boy again, terrified and full of dread, until the fires went out and all that remained was a deformed, weathered skull sitting in a puddle of flesh. I screamed, scrambling backwards until my back hit the trunk of the pine I had been camped under. As if it were real, I felt the scratch of the bark through my clothes, its unyielding firmness as the battle raged around me.

I closed my eyes, praying that I would return from whatever hell I'd fallen into, and blindly reached for the bottle of laudanum I had dropped while crawling away in fright. As soon as my hand closed around the comforting coolness of the bottle, the din around me abruptly ceased. The scent of battle and of blood dissipated until all I could smell was the sharpness of the pines, the moist soil, and the petrichor of the rain. When I opened my eyes, my fire had long since gone out, and I was back in the Brașov Forest of the present day.

I continued to tremble while packing up my sparse camp. It wasn't until I was striding away toward the fog-enshrouded keep that I could finally address my horrible dream. Clearly, the combination of the laudanum I had drunk as well as the history and legends surrounding Fort Brașov had merged in my tired brain to create the scene that had disturbed me so. I've never had such a realistic dream, and as I made my way to the bottom of the small, bare mountain that held the fort, I was deeply unsettled.

At the bottom of the rocky hill the keep perched atop, the road widened, unencumbered by the creeping forest. I stepped out onto a relatively flat surface and trudged up the long road that circled towards the crumbling walls on top of the hill. Out of the shelter of the trees, the wind blew with a ferocity that plastered my damp clothes to my skin, and in that moment, I was certain I would never be warm again. When I finally arrived, cold, miserable and sore, at the summit, I was barely able to take in the stunning view of both the fort and the forest below me.

The walls of the fort were an old and weathered stone, surprisingly devoid of any lichen or moss, scoured both by time and the relentless wind. I touched the stone, expecting to feel some awe-inspiring sense of the history and bloodshed that had gone into the making of these walls, but I felt nothing but rock, cold and indifferent to my presence. It was a rather disappointing moment, and I hunched my shoulders in irritation and sullenly made my way into the ancient ruin. It was decrepit in many places, the walls tilting inwards or having collapsed entirely into piles of rubble.

There were many corridors and sets of winding stairs that led up, higher into the fort, but I was so tired and cold at that point that I dragged myself into a room where the ceiling remained intact. The wind whistled fiercely outside, and I relished finding such a quiet nook. There wasn't much to be found in the way of tinder, but the idea of a fire's warmth spurred me and I found several pieces of furniture when I explored deeper into the fort, and I dragged them behind me and broke the rotted wood down with several well-placed kicks. My fingers shook as I used my flint, but after several attempts, a spark finally landed on the wood and caught. I carefully built the fire up, but the small room soon filled with smoke, and I realized I had built it in the wrong place. I found another room with a small window and started the process over again with the fire directly below the opening. Small gusts of wind made their way in, but it worked in my favour, and I soon had a fire crackling merrily. The warmth, coupled with my exhaustion and a headache that lingered after the previous night, had a soporific effect, and I drifted off to sleep, huddled beneath my blanket and using my pack as a pillow.

The sleep, thankfully, was a deep and dreamless one. When I woke, I was surprisingly restored and came into awareness abruptly. It was with no small amount of shock that I realized I was not alone.

A figure sat on the other side of my still-burning campfire, wreathed in flame. It took me a moment to realize it was a woman, and that it was just the angle at which I viewed her that made it seem as if she were surrounded by a halo of flame. She was as solid as I was, sitting there on her knees. When she held her hands out near the fire, the light and shadow flickered across them. When she noticed I was awake, her serious face softened into a beatific smile.

She was stunningly beautiful—her features seemingly carved from the finest white marble. She brushed her long, dark, wavy hair back from her face, revealing deep blue eyes—highly unusual in this area where muddled brown and dull greens were the norm. She smiled with her whole being, a bright ray of sunshine in a miserable place, and she still had all of her teeth; in fact, they were white and clean, and framed so nicely by her plump, red lips that I found myself utterly enchanted.

She wore a thick cloak with a mantle of wolf's fur, and when she shifted, I saw a glimpse of a deep indigo fabric. We stared at each other for a moment over the flames—she, still smiling softly at me, and myself, completely addled by the unexpected appearance of such an angelic creature.

"Sorry to disturb you," she said in a low, musical voice. "I could smell your fire and couldn't help but want to warm myself by it. I hope it's not a problem." She had a mild and pleasant accent, but I found myself unable to place it.

"Y-you are more than welcome to it," I stuttered. "I was unaware anyone still lived at the fort—I hope I am not intruding."

She laughed then. "The fort is not exactly home. My home is a distance away, but I have lingered here for some time now."

"Are you here alone?" I asked with some concern. "A lady such as yourself should not be here alone without companionship or aid."

"Not quite, though I'm not sure where my companion is at the moment. It has been a while since I have seen him," she said. "Luckily, I am well enough acquainted with the fort and the surrounding area that I can manage just fine. Who are you? What are you doing here?"

I gave her my name and how I had come to visit the fort on my journey trekking through the countries littering the main mountain range that crossed the map of the area like an angry gash in the world.

"I'm Marita," she said. "It is a pleasure to meet you."

"The pleasure is all mine," I said fervently. "If you would excuse me for one moment, I'll return as quickly as I can."

She smiled at me, and I hurried outside to where a fierce wind was still blowing, and quickly relieved myself. I looked up at the sky with some trepidation. While it was not raining yet, the clouds were heavy and low, and in the distance I thought I could see lightning light up a cloud from within.

When I returned, she had moved herself so that she sat on my blanket, and she patted the rumpled spot beside her. I acquiesced and moved to sit beside her. Up close, she was even more of an exquisite creature, with long dark lashes and peerless skin. I could not stop myself from staring, which she gratefully did not acknowledge.

"Tell me," she said. "About the place that you come from?"

My stomach growled then, loudly and insistently, and I dug through my pack for the last meager crumbs of my provisions. I handed her some, which she took gravely and began to nibble on. As we ate, I told her more about my family. She was an attentive listener, asking the right questions at the right time, encouraging me to share more and more. I would occasionally become distracted by her beauty, but she would gently steer me back on track, asking me many questions about my home and history.

"I have never been so far away from here," she said after I had given a detailed description of the manse in the countryside where my family summered and she had exclaimed how beautiful it all sounded. "The fort is the farthest I have ever been away from home, and even then it is not so far."

"Do you plan on traveling when your companion returns?" I asked her. There was a flicker of fear in her eyes.

"I often hope that he never returns," she said softly. "He is not a kind man."

My heart broke for her at that moment, and without thinking about it, I turned to her and gathered up her small hands in my own. They were cold, and I resisted the urge to blow on them and warm them. "I am so sorry," I murmured. "What can I do to assist you?"

Her eyes lit up, giving my hands a light squeeze, but no response. We sat there for a moment, our hands still clasped together, staring deep into each other's eyes, before she broke the silence.

"Would you like a tour of the fort? Or what remains of it? I know some of its history and layout, having been here for so long."

I didn't want our moment of quiet intimacy to end, but I nodded. She stood then, and I followed after her. She barely came up to my chest. While I was taller than the average man back home, she was truly petite, doll-sized, even. Her stature and vulnerability made my heart swell with a fierce protective desire.

She led me deeper into the fort, and as we picked our way around the debris and collapsed walls, she pointed out small rooms or ruined sections and told me what they had once been. A pantry, a closet, an office, an armory. We came to a large room where the small passages swelled into a grand space. A lot of half-rotted wood littered the ground, and at the end of the room towered a massive fireplace, filled with soot and half-dead leaves.

"This was the great hall where everyone gathered for meals. Many men died here during the final siege," she said, though there were no signs of any skeletal remains.

As I gazed around the room, it was as if another image became overlaid on it. I could see it as it was back then—the floor scattered with pine needles, a fire roaring in the great hearth as dark and dangerous men sat at long, rough-hewn tables, arguing amongst themselves. Here and there, large rangy dogs darted in and out, snarling at each other as the men dropped scraps and bones onto the floor below. At the far end, there was a large dark throne, and upon it a shadowy figure sat, robed in thick furs. At his feet was a stool, and sitting upon it was a small and similarly shadowed figure.

I blinked, and the image dissolved. She was staring at me, and I shook my head.

"I have an overactive imagination," I told her. "I was picturing how it must have been back then."

"It was not a pleasant place," she said grimly. "This whole place was filled with the bloodlust of men and their thirst for power and possessions. I am convinced the horror and the sin of it all has sunk into the walls, down into the very earth, and mixed with the soil in such a way that the area will never be able to rid itself of that terrible legacy." She trembled as she spoke, and I moved to take one of her hands again. She allowed it.

"Do not trouble yourself with such horrible thoughts," I said to her. "You are far too beautiful to be thinking about such gruesome things and the squabbles of dead men."

She blushed, and I could not help but admire the pretty shade of pink her cheeks flushed, and I told her so. She laughed then and smiled at me.

"Come," she said. "There is one more place that I would show you." She led me to a narrow staircase. We climbed until my legs and lungs burned, walking down hallways to different sets of stairs that twisted and turned and climbed higher and higher. The fort had been a maze even before it had begun to collapse, and it was even more so now. Large portions of the floor were missing, and many of the walls were dangerously crumbling, but her footsteps were sure against the floor and she led without hesitation. I followed, trusting her implicitly. Finally, we came to the remains of another door, and she moved out onto a small battlement. One half of it had tumbled down the hillside, but we hung back on the part that remained.

"This is where they killed him," she said stonily. "Removed his head from his body and placed it on a pole so that it could look out at the expanse of what had once been his domain." The wind buffeted us. Her dark hair blew behind her, and I thought to myself that if all flags were so beautiful, I could imagine marching to war behind one. She looked like a creature out of myth.

The expanse of the Brașov Forest lay spread before us. In the distance, I could make out a spot where the trees ended and where the town must have begun. Above us, the sky roiled, dark clouds rushing over each other and tumbling like a litter of puppies.

"There's a terrible storm coming, I think," I said. "We should get back inside before it hits. We should also find food and firewood so that we may shelter through it in comfort."

She stared up at the storm, her eyes glazed. I reached out to touch her, and she drew back with a start. I apologized for frightening her, and she waved away my words with a smile.

"I'll lead the way," she said, and we began the twisting journey back to the main floor and to the room where the fire waited for us. We split up then—she said she had a number of traps set and teased me that a strapping young man like myself must need a fair amount of food. I preened under her compliments and went to gather firewood from the rooms I had noted during our earlier exploration and stacked it against the far wall of what I hoped would now be "our" room.

She brought me a brace of wild rabbits, and together we skinned them, skewered them, and roasted them over the flame, their blood dripping down to land with a sizzle on the embers. We ate them like that, fat dripping down our chins, laughing at the absurdity of it all. It was clear to me the lady was of a high and refined breeding, based on her beauty, her composure, and her manners, and I quickly became enamored even more with each passing moment. We passed the remaining bit of laudanum back and forth, giggling and sipping from it.

"How are we ever going to clean ourselves up?" I wondered aloud after we had both eaten our fill. Our hands and faces were covered in the remains of our dinner, our skin shiny and slick with grease. Marita looked with a devilish grin at me and stood up. Her skin was flushed and she removed her cloak with a flourish, revealing the deep blue shift underneath it. She was as shapely as she was beautiful, and I caught my breath as I beheld her.

She ran through the door, leaving me sitting there, drunk and more than a little stunned. She laughed and called back to me, and I followed. By the time I caught up with her, she was standing in front of the door I had initially entered from. I approached her with a question on my lips, but she hushed me, standing up on her tiptoes and laying a small and slender finger against my mouth. She smiled somewhat wickedly, and then she dragged me out into the pouring rain. Laughing, the two of us began drunkenly washing our hands and faces in the downpour. I laughed as she twirled and danced in it, clapping my hands to the beat her feet made against the muddy earth in synchronization with the rain. Suddenly, she reached up to grasp me by the shirt collars and dragged me down for a kiss, her soft lips grazing mine. I froze for a moment, and then my arms were around her and I was kissing her, and kissing her hard.

Our tongues warred with each other. I could taste the alcohol and opium upon her breath and did my best to steal it away from her. I crushed her to me, lifting her slender form until her legs wrapped around my waist. She moaned and ground against my hardening desire, and I swore under my breath as she kissed and nibbled her way up on my neck and jawline before sucking my earlobe into her mouth. My stomach tightened, and as the rain pounded against us, I pushed her up against a wall, my hands fumbling with her buttons and laces.

Her clothes now clung to her, revealing every single perfect detail of her voluptuous body. I went down to my knees, my mouth upon her breasts as I finally peeled her sodden dress off of her. She stood there in the pouring rain, a goddess unashamed. She raised me back off of my knees and drew my lips back to hers as her clever fingers yanked my pants down impatiently. My hands cupped her perfect bottom. I pushed her up and held her against the wall, my fingers searching for her slick opening until I was able to guide myself in.

I sunk myself into her hot embrace, moaning, and her breath hitched as I plunged desperately into her, my mind blanking as I felt such an overwhelming need that I lost myself. I thrust into her roughly, with no rhythm, and her hips somehow managed to match mine every time as we careened towards a mutual climax. The two of us cried out as thunder rumbled overhead, and I leaned against the wall, spent. She softly kissed my chest over and over. I could feel myself already growing hard again and quickly disengaged. We gathered up our things, rushing back to our room to continue our activities together in a drier and warmer climate.

The night was a blur. Our lovemaking fluctuated between slow and sensual, and frantic and lustful. We stopped now and then to doze, or continue to pass the now nearly empty bottle back and forth. My memory became hazy at one point. I recall a moment like a dream, where she lay still on my chest, still straddling me while I remained inside of her. "Will you take me with you? When you leave?" she asked, her voice low and satiated.

"Of course," I said.

"Do you promise?"

I kissed her and told her that wherever I would go, she now went too. She kissed me with a level of desperation I didn't understand at the time, and we had begun to move our bodies in harmony again. Outside, the storm raged, but we were so wrapped up in each other we were incapable of noticing it. We fell into a sleep in the deep of the night, exhausted by our obsession with one another. It was a deep sleep, a contented sleep, and I wish I had enjoyed it all the more knowing that I would never have one such as that again.

She woke me in the morning—or at least I think it was the morning. The sky was still dark and angry, the rain coming down in sheets, but it was perceptibly lighter despite the horrible gloom. She grasped my shoulder roughly and shook me awake.

"He's coming," she said, her eyes wide and panicked. "He's coming."

"Who is coming? Your companion?" I said groggily.

"My husband," she whispered, and in her wide eyes I saw the reflection of flames leaping. It startled me, for our fire had turned to embers that barely now glowed in the dim of the room.

"Your husband?" I whispered, now wide awake. "What do you mean, your husband?" I'm sure there was a hurt and plaintive whine to my voice as I felt a rather ridiculous sting of betrayal.

"He's coming," she said again urgently and with no further explanation scrambled upright. The strong and confident woman was gone, and in her place was a girl who looked terrified out of her wits. She did not bother to dress but darted out the door in a panic, naked. Alarmed, I gathered up my still-damp pants from their place by the fire and followed, shoving my feet through them as I stumbled out the door.

"Marita!" I cried into the dark of the fort's interior. "Marita!" I could hear her begin to weep and followed the sound of it. I caught a glimpse then of her pale skin up ahead as she darted into a room. I moved to follow.

Something roared then, something dark and old and angry. It sent the hair along my bare arms rising, and my heart dropped into my stomach. There came a deep rumbling, and the floors shook as if hell itself was opening up beneath them. There was a brief moment of silence, and then Marita screamed, loud and shrill, and then she was there running towards me, her face slack with fear, arms and legs flailing wildly in her panic.

"Marita! What is going on?!" I cried, grabbing at her arm as she moved to pass me. I wrapped my arms around her, but even as I did, she drew back her hand and slapped me. My face burned and stung where her small palm had struck it, and she took several steps backwards. She stared at me as if I were a stranger, so numb and stark with terror that she had no idea who I was. She turned and fled again as another roar sounded, and as she disappeared from my line of sight, the thing chasing her stalked into view.

It was tall—twice as tall as a man, and it ducked as it entered the room. Despite its burly bulk, thick chest and muscular, practically bulbous, arms, it moved with a deadly and volatile grace as it stalked after the distressed woman. Its muscular torso tapered down to the legs and hooves like those of an ox or a goat—I could not decide then, nor now, whether it reminded me more of a creature out of Greek mythology or one out of Christian theology. Heat rolled off of its skin in waves, and despite my near-nudity and the brisk night air, sweat beaded on my skin almost immediately.

It continued to chase her, practically sauntering as it followed after her. It turned to look at me as it passed, and with a sense of growing horror, I realized it was the distorted face from my dream in the forest—the man turned monster following his death. The cheekbones were still high and pulled back from a mouth of razor fangs, and those twin horns emerged from a thick and heavy brow. The eyes—the eyes haunt me still. They were pits—dark holes filled with flames, and when I looked into them, I could see figures writhing in the flames in silent agony. It bellowed again, and I couldn't stop myself from beginning to cry, tears streaming down my face.

It grinned then, delighted by my terror, but it did not pause in its pursuit of Marita.

I stood for a moment in shock as it disappeared through the doorway. At some point, Marita's screams roused me to action, and I tore after them, following their footsteps and respective shouts as Marita led the monster on a cat-and-mouse chase through the labyrinthine fort.

I got turned around at some point, and somehow exited the castle into the pouring rain. I was about to dive back in when I caught a glimpse of white at the uppermost parapet, where Marita and I had stood mere hours before.

"Marita!" I screamed. "Marita!" The wind tore the words from my throat as I tried to hoarsely call her name over and over again. The droplets of cold rain were like icy daggers being driven into my skin by the hateful wind, but the temperature could not rival the cold that crept over me as I realized what was about to occur.

I could not see the exact events as they unfolded, but I have dwelled on them for so long and with such obsession that I can see them in my mind's eye. Marita stood at the edge of the half-collapsed parapet, her dark hair whipping around her head like a halo of shifting shadows. She stared down at the woods, at the thrashing branches, and the lightning that arced its way across the sky, and realized she had nowhere left to run.

Behind her, the devil squeezed itself through the last door. It opened its mouth, and its words were mangled by its fangs. "*Marita*," it said in a sibilant hiss. "*Marita*." She looked at it, and it must have grinned at her, reaching one hand out to snatch at her with fingers tipped with sharp and bloody claws. She barely paused to think about it, but threw herself over the parapet, her body a flash of white against the angry sky as she tumbled into the churning dark, her final wail echoing through the rain as she plunged to her death.

I will never forget the horrible sound of her hitting the earth in front of me. The strange wetness of it, the crunch of her breaking bones, the noise her skull made as it struck the ground like an overripe apple, the pulp of it spattering across the stone.

I remained there mutely, gaping at her corpse. I could not bring myself to touch her—she was so broken and bloody and battered that she was unrecognizable from the delicate creature I had held in my arms an hour before. She was a porcelain doll smashed beyond repair.

Above us on the parapet, the devil stood unbothered by the storm or the death of my beloved. He turned his flaming eyes upon me, his long sharp teeth bared in a grin that promised terrible violence, saliva dripping down that jutting and skeletal chin. At that moment, everything became too much, and my fear trickled down my leg to mix with the rain in a puddle at my feet. The devil lifted a finger, pointing at me with such promise that I knew if he caught me, I would suffer horribly before I died at his hands.

I fled then, down the ancient road, down into the forest and into the raging storm. I crashed through the underbrush in a panic, sobbing for Marita and for my mother. From above me, through the din of thunder and terrible wind, I heard the devil bellow again and again and again as if in triumph, until both the trees and distance muffled the sound of the storm and the nightmare that stalked it.

I had a fever dream of a week lost in Brașov Forest, tortured and taunted by visions of devils and dead women. I somehow managed to find my way back and stumbled into Brașov, delirious with exhaustion and fever, starved, dehydrated, and suffering from severe exposure. With my flair for the dramatic, it is no surprise that I collapsed in the middle of the town square during a market day, and many rough hands ferried me to the doctor where I lay insensible for several days. When I awoke to a heavy scolding from the local leech on my idiocy, I quickly cut them off and told them my tale, with a few details omitted for posterity. I only told them of a woman of unknown origin whom I had found living in the fort, and who, in the middle of that particularly bad storm, had slipped and fallen to her death from the fort's walls.

I begged them to go and retrieve her body, but they said that no one, much less a woman, could survive in a crumbling ruin like that without having at some point made their way into the village for supplies. I insisted again and again, and they questioned me, and when I mentioned the bottle of absinthe that Marita and I had shared together, he met the eyes of the innkeeper. From that moment on, they dismissed me and my experiences.

While I recovered, I asked for any knowledge of the fort itself to be brought to me so I could research the devil that haunted its halls as I continued to convalesce. There wasn't much, but the local monastery did have several scrolls and pieces of paper detailing the construction of the fort. In one of them, one of the chief stonecutters had written to his wife in town to talk of a wedding between the warlord and a lady of renowned beauty he had brought in from a neighboring country. He had done a drawing of the newlywed couple for his wife, and when my eyes fell upon it, my heart stopped beating in my chest.

It was a rough sketch, but even without the benefit of colour or detail, I could see the outline of my beloved's face, the jawline I had tenderly traced with kisses, the high-arched brows that I had admired. Next to her stood a man with small, angry eyes, and thick, shaggy black hair that hung past his shoulders.

When my next meal came, I begged the innkeeper's wife to talk to me so I could know more about the warlord and the woman in the sketch. I insisted, pressing for details from the reticent woman, who had only crossed herself and fled the room. I lay there, frustrated and thwarted, until there was a knock at the door a quarter hour later.

It was a black-robed priest. He glowered at me and asked why I would frighten that poor woman with my ramblings and questions about a history best left buried. Although I apologized for scaring the poor woman, I confessed of my experience at the fort that defied explanation, and while he cocked a shaggy and stern brow at me, he did not say a word as I told him my story. When I had finished, I pressed him for details about the history of Fort Braşov, and this time he did not refuse.

The warlord, he said, had been considered a demon or the devil himself, depending on who you asked. People did not go to the fort or live there because they were convinced it was cursed, as was the forest itself. I begged him to tell me the warlord's name, but he said it had been erased from history and from memory in the belief that if his name was uttered, it would bring the devil down upon the forest again.

"Had he had a wife?" I asked with fervor. "Children?"

He'd had a wife, yes, whose name he did not recall, but there had never been any children, and thank the Lord for that. The marriage had been a dark and unhappy one, and when a *voivode* had visited to discuss an alliance and the lending of troops, the voivode had brought his teenage son. In her desperation to escape, the wife had seduced the young man and made him promise to take her away from the fort by sneaking her away within his father's train of courtiers. The young man had begun to make arrangements with some of the servants, but the warlord became suspicious and had burst in upon the young man and his wife *inflagrante delicto.* The warlord had immediately drawn his weapon and run the voivode's son through while she was still in his arms, creating a shallow wound in her stomach. She had run naked and screaming through the halls, covered in her own blood and the blood of her unfortunate lover, while her furious husband chased her. She had fled up one of the winding staircases, and when she reached the top, her husband close on her heels, she flung herself from the walls of the fort rather than fall into his clutches. Her body had been recovered the next morning, broken and bashed beyond recognition, and burned.

The death of the voivode's son, as well as the ensuing chaos, had been the trigger for the series of events that led to the lord's eventual downfall and demise. I sent the priest away with a thank you and stared up at the ceiling, numb, for the rest of the afternoon.

Once I further recovered, I sent two young men to the fort to retrieve my pack. They left early the next morning and returned before sunset, and I bitterly paid them from my emergency money before booking the next carriage out of town. I did not ask if they had found Marita's body—I knew that any part of her that remained had long ago been turned to ash and scattered by the brutal winds.

I headed home, straight as an arrow, only stopping to eat, piss, and switch transportation. I preferred to catch small bits and pieces of slumber in the carriage. The jostling of the seats made it impossible for me to fall into a deep enough sleep that I could dream, and for that I was grateful, because when I did dream, I dreamed of her.

There were two dreams that haunted me then and still haunt me now. Sleep has become a terror, and I spend most of my nights avoiding it, at a severe detriment to my health. It has been years since I trekked through the mountains and valleys of Eastern Europe, but time and distance have done nothing to ease the nightmares that torture me when I close my eyes. I have consulted dozens of doctors, and besides prescriptions for laudanum or whispers of where I could find a more reputable opium den, none have been able to rid me of my visions.

The first dream begins hazily. Marita and I are back in the small room I called home for those few days. We are tangled up in each other, and the room spins as she rides me, her hips grinding into mine as she drives me deeper and deeper into her core, her head thrown back in ecstasy. She stops for a moment on the precipice of pleasure and looks down at me. Everything is suddenly thrown into sharp relief as her body begins to distort. Bones suddenly break and jut through her skin, blood spurting and sprinkling down on me like a warm spring rain. Her thighs tighten, holding me in place so that I can not move as she continues to move against me.

"Take me away from here," she says, her blue eyeball dangling down against her cheekbone, her words slurred as she continues pumping. I am frozen in place, torn between pleasure and terror, unable to do much of anything but stare as bits of brain matter drip down through her hair. "Please, take me away from here."

She finishes with a scream like the one that tore from her throat as she jumped to her death, and I awake in a cold sweat, a sticky trail of fear and desire drying on my thighs as I curl up and cry.

The other dream occurs every time it rains, whether it be a gentle drizzle, a spot of rain, a violent downpour, and I can no longer hold off the sleep that threatens me. I am careening through those horrible halls, trying to find my way to Marita, my way out, my way to anything. The walls fall in on me, shrinking and growing as I stumble through them, crying and pleading for direction. The shrieks of my love and the monstrous sounds of her husband echo as he pursues her through the decaying halls, and I am so very lost and so very alone as I scramble after the two of them, hoping to stop the horrible thing that is about to happen, but nothing ever changes, and she leaps from the parapet again and again and again.

I awake more drained and tired than before. I am so weary now, as if my soul has been tied to an anchor that is falling into a fathomless abyss. More often now than not, I wonder about ending it all, about marching to the very top of my father's house and throwing myself off of the uppermost balcony, finally ending the horrors that I experienced there in the fort and continue to experience every time I close my eyes. What else is left for me? Whether alive or dead, I will forever be a man burdened by the long memory of Braşov, haunted by the horrors of the past and forever cursed to follow in the footsteps of ghosts.

KUMBAYA

In the trash-filled narrow streets of the city, someone is singing. Down the dark alleyway filled with diseased rats, their claws scratching against the cobblestone, a thin voice can be heard, a toneless lullaby hummed by an old woman. In her arms, she clutches a bundle of stained and greasy rags bound in the shape of a child. Arthritic hands stroke the face of the doll lovingly, swollen knuckles brushing against it in the imitation of motherhood. She rocks back and forth in a rhythmic manner. Her eyes are glazed with cataracts, her face bursting with pustulant sores. Liquid erupts from one of these rotting volcanoes, trickling down her weathered face like a tear, dripping down onto her "child's" face. She absentmindedly wipes it away and continues humming.

The halls of the asylum echo with crazed laughter, a house of clowns for the lords' amusement. They strut through Bedlam, knocking against the cages of the zoo, inciting the inmates to further madness. The ladies cover their noses with scented handkerchiefs while the men guffaw and

point out ragged and cowering inmates. They pause before a cell. In it, a man sits in the corner, filthy, giggling to himself as he slowly rips out his own fingernails. A well-dressed woman muffles a horrified scream, the men chatter to themselves, and the group moves on, eager to continue their tour.

Someone's crying, my Lord, Kumbaya

In the nearly empty church, the specter of a heavily pregnant young woman moves up the aisle, her muddy feet leaving a trail of filth behind her. She clutches her rags closer around her as she stumbles towards the altar. She cradles her swollen belly as a forbidding figure dressed in a black cowl moves from the shadows to confront her, standing before the altar and refusing her plea to light a candle for her unborn child. The priest hisses at the softly weeping woman, pushing her away and roughly grabbing her arm and shoving her out the door. She lands on her stomach and curls into the fetal position, still crying. Snow begins to fall, melting on her pale and exposed skin.

Someone's praying, my Lord, Kumbaya

The family huddles around the child's sickbed, hands clasped so hard the knuckles have turned white. His rattling breaths are becoming further and further apart. The blush of his fever has faded, and his whitened lips are painted red by each gasping cough. His mother reaches over tenderly to wipe the blood away with a crimson-stained cloth. Crying to herself, his sister sits on the stool in her threadbare skirts. His father kneels by the bed, clutching at the bed-sheets as his lips move in a silent frenzy. A cold wind gusts through the ramshackle house, creating a whirlwind of scattered Bible pages and debris. It exits through the cracks of the wooden shutters of the small square windows, taking the child with it, leaving behind a sobbing mother and a still feverishly praying father.

Someone's sleeping, my Lord, Kumbaya

He is lying half in, half out of the street, his ragged workman's clothes stained with soot and coal, a dribble of orange vomit trickling down a greasy, unshaved chin. People move past him in the dark, stepping over his broken-doll limbs, covering their noses with handkerchiefs spritzed with perfume at the rank smell of alcohol mixed with sweat radiating off the man like a furnace gives off heat. A gentleman waves over a police officer, pointing at the unconscious man. The police officer kicks the prone figure and shrugs at the gentleman, who walks on.

In the gutter, the man throws up on himself.

Oh Lord, Kumbaya

CONTENT WARNINGS

animal death
birth-related trauma
body horror including extreme mutilation
cannibalism
child death
child endangerment, violence, and abuse
cruelty toward disabled peoples
cruelty toward elderly
cruelty toward mental asylum patients
dental trauma
drug use
forced marriage
loss of a child, parent, and/or partner

Hannah Birss (she/her) is a widely-published writer and aspiring magpie based out of Ontario, Canada. She lives with her partner, children, and multiple animals in a nest constructed from books and various trinkets. In addition to a multitude of short stories and anthologies, Hannah's full-length works include *From Damsels Into Dragons* and *Bigfoot in Love and Other Stories*.

Upcoming works include:
Silver & Gold
Tongue in Cheek, Eyes in Sockets (middlegrade horror)
A Love Like Sharp Teeth
Saltwater Sorrows
Old Bones Funny Bones

Follow her on Instagram or Threads @hannahbirsswrites or visit her at www.hannahbirsswrites.ca for upcoming publishing news and various nonsense.

Thank you for supporting Graveside Press and our authors. One of the biggest ways you can help is to leave a star rating or a review wherever you purchased your copy!

STAY SPOOKY.

Remember, you can buy books directly from us for cheaper!
gsp-shop.fourthwall.com/admin/dashboard

Wanna come hang out with the ghouls?
gravesidepress.carrd.co

Stay up to date with Graveside news and exclusive stories.
graveside-press.com